Praise for
THE TRUTH ABOUT WHITE LIES

"A brave and searing deep dive into white supremacy from the side of the privileged."

—NIC STONE,
New York Times bestselling author of *Dear Martin*

"A brilliant, riveting page-turner. Cole has flawlessly crafted an addicting story about the depths and domino effect of white supremacy."

—TIFFANY D. JACKSON,
bestselling author of *Grown* and *White Smoke*

"A vicious, incendiary novel, told with clarity and precision. . . . Unforgettable."

—MARK OSHIRO,
award-winning author of *Anger Is a Gift*

"This is brilliant, brutal, and essential reading for all."

—ASHLEY WOODFOLK,
acclaimed author of *The Beauty That Remains*

"Brilliant, urgent, and profoundly honest—this is the kind of novel that knocks on the door of your heart and demands to know who you are."

—BRENDAN KIELY,
New York Times bestselling coauthor of *All American Boys*
and *The Other Talk: Reckoning with Our White Privilege*

"This is absolutely necessary work."

—KIESE LAYMON,
award-winning author of *Heavy*

Dear Medusa

OLIVIA A. COLE

 LABYRINTH ROAD | NEW YORK

Visit us on the Web! GetUnderlined.com

Educators and librarians, for a variety of teaching tools, visit us at RHTeachersLibrarians.com

Library of Congress Cataloging-in-Publication Data is available upon request.
ISBN 978-0-593-48573-6 (trade)—ISBN 978-0-593-48575-0 (ebook)

The text of this book is set in 10.75-point Adobe Garamond Pro.
Interior design by Jen Valero

Printed in the United States of America
10 9 8 7 6 5 4 3
First Edition

Random House Children's Books supports the First Amendment and celebrates the right to read.

For me.
And for you.
And for all of us.

The worst part of working fast food is the name tag

because there's always somebody's mom with coupons
who thinks they are somehow being cheated by the teenager
at the register, and their eyes always dart down
to your chest to look for a way to be in charge.

"Listen," she says, and I see her eyes laser in,
search out my name.
"*Alicia*. You overcharged me for my mozzarella sticks. Now,
do I need to ask for the manager or are you going to make it right?"

Make it right. Ever since last year, everything
sounds like justice or
its burning absence.

She thinks she's been done grievous wrong
by the two dollars extra on her waxy receipt
and my mouth is supposed to be apologizing
but my mind is on everything else:

• the whole school/world calling me a whore
• Sarah cutting me out of her life like a tumor
• my parents, the wood chipper of their life between them

In the end I just say, "Ma'am, I'll do my best.
I'll do my very best."

We both know
she'll still call the manager over,
will still make the world a witness
to all the things she thinks she deserves
even with my smile so bright
it shatters.

It's my last weekday shift before school

and it's just girls on the clock, no creepy manager,
no too-old guys pretending they're still in high school
and eyeing you over curly fries.

Slow day. No construction workers,
no cops expecting free food,
no guys in suits who refuse coupons
because they want you to know
they're rich:

just teenage girls who don't go
to the same school,

carrying different gossip
    not about each other
and thus unimportant.

Stephanie is the shift manager
and she's only twenty-one so
when there's no customers
she lets us turn up the lobby music
and all of us sing along.

The final day of August is like a guillotine

separating September from the rest of the summer
in one clean slice, the red sun bleeding out
over my feet as I circle the school
in my Meat Palace uniform
one more time before I start junior year.

It's empty. No one but me
would ever come to school while the freedom

summer drops like gold confetti
still sparkles on our shoulders.

But I like it like this, the quiet, the way
the beige bricks drink up the sunset,
taking on a color that reminds me
of a desert. Dry, baked,
vicious.

I've never been anywhere but here.

My feet take me to the track, like they miss it.
Maybe they do. Maybe they remember
how it felt to transform
from girl to mustang
with grateful lungs heaving.

Freshman year
I could fly.

Then sophomore year happened.

I look back at the pink bricks,
settling into a deeper shade
now that the sun is sinking.

I'm sinking too, down onto the bleachers,

the metal warm against my thighs.
This school is empty of people
and full of memories
and I don't want
any of them.

My mother offers to iron my school uniform and even though I want her to, I say no,

because sometimes
    in this place
    where I am

it feels good to refuse
help, because saying yes
to even something like an iron

feels like saying yes
    to everything else

when my whole life
has become a pipe bomb
full of pieces
that explode in a furious
    no.

TUESDAY, SEPTEMBER 4
The school bus stops on my block but I don't get on.

I've been taking the city bus all summer
and I like the way it makes me feel
like I'm living in a different world
than the people who are supposed to be
my peers. What's the difference?

At least on the city bus
I can pull the string,
and it makes me feel
like I'm in control.

I can get off whenever I want
wherever I want
even if my destination
is predetermined.

On the city bus I can still wonder
what the people there think about me,
whereas at school
once I walk through the door
I already know what they're all thinking,
what they're all going
to say
about all the versions of me they think they know,
laid alongside
all the girls I was before
in stark contrast.

Flashbacks

They are like ripples on a pond and they begin
in my earliest memories of myself:

Playing in the fountains at Elwain Park
with no shirt on, five-year-old bird
chest

Eight and pointing at bras in Target, my brother
wearing them like hats while my mother
shopped and I laughed

Sarah getting her first bikini, me ten
and silent and feeling a brand-new envy
grow in like ivy

Me eleven
Me twelve
Me thirteen
Me fourteen

Curious and curious
Me warming up
Me sneaking to buy my first thong
Me excited for someone
    anyone
to notice

Me kissing Michael Strong
the day I got my braces off
just to feel what someone's tongue felt like
sliding across new teeth

Me hearing about what good girls
do and think and say
and always feeling like a neon opposite
even if only in shadow.

Me thinking I had secrets until last year
when I learned what it meant—
    what it really meant—
to hide.

There's always a white kid who says
"Why do the Black kids sit together in
the cafeteria? They segregate themselves."

And I'm a white girl too so what do I know
but I think the answer is so obvious in a school as white

as this one
where Halloween parties still feature blackface and redface
where the student council only barely voted
(5–6)
to maintain a special events calendar for Black History Month
and the cheerleading squad is all white but shouts *yas queen, werk!*
    between routines.

Dawn of Day 1
and we're all in the cafeteria waiting to be dismissed,
the swell of the student body heaving as if on a ship at rough sea,
all of us deciding where we fit, where to squeeze in, if anyone we
    hate or love
has rendered certain sections unsittable.

The girl who says it this year is skinny and blond,
a sophomore, and her whole table murmurs and laughs,
casts glances at the three tables where the couple dozen Black
    students,
the half-dozen kids from Mexico and El Salvador,
all take refuge in each other's presence.

Why wouldn't they

when to sit anywhere else in this sea of narrowed eyes and fake laughs
would be like throwing yourself overboard?

I'd never say that I consider my pain equal
but I can say I know
how it feels to step onto a ship
and be confident that everyone on board
is watching you, thinking that you're not a sailor
but a creature from the deep.

The only text messages I get are from coworkers.

Mariah: can you take my shift tomorrow

Alicia: what time

Mariah: 3:30

Mariah: . . . ?

Alicia: I'm in school, sorry. Yes I'll take it.

Mariah: I thought you were dropping out

Alicia: I wish

And from random dudes.

Him: Thinking about you

Alicia: I know what that means

Him: yeah;)

Him: free tonight?

Alicia: tomorrow

Day 1 was a success

in the way that surviving a haunted house
is a success:

I walked through the halls and saw
lots of ghosts

but never
the Devil
himself.

The garage is full of smoke

and someone who doesn't live in this gray
house might think something is on fire.

If they looked closer they would know nothing
is, the smoke they see only the last remains
of what has finally ceased to burn. What's left
of my family is a cold smolder. Divorce
is only white-hot for so long. If you've ever watched a fire
you know it eventually gives way to a gray zero,
smoke coming from nothing, piles of ash.

The smoke is my mother sitting in a lawn chair
cigarette in hand, coffee can next to her for the ashes.
She talks to her mother
or her sister
sometimes a friend from college
and from where I stand in the kitchen
I can hear the low blur of her voice,
the clink of the can when she taps,
the slide of a beer across the concrete.
It's only the two of us.

My brother and my father have become
heavy apparitions. They exist but on a different
plane. My mother is here with me but she's
also somewhere else—on nights like tonight
the garage is a distant universe
I would need time travel to cross.
Sometimes I stand at the door and try to listen
while my leftovers spin in the microwave.

Occasionally she laughs,
but mostly she cries.

My parents met when my father was still mid-divorce

with his first wife, one child already somewhere
in Montana.
He was 31 and my mother 20
and she was dancing at a college party
when he saw her,
her hair the same black as fresh asphalt
but softer, and swinging,
and he never danced
but that night he danced for her
the way birds in the wild
spread feathers and perform.

But like geese
and not doves,
my father takes many mates
and even when my mother still waxes
romantic about love at first sight
(even now)
and the way the music slowed
when their eyes met,
sometimes I wonder
(since the divorce)
what he was doing at that party
in the first place.

Portrait of a day

Dawn and toast.

Bus and its flickering yellow light.

School and its silent rivers of judgment.

Boys and their fingers in my belt loops
even when we don't know each other.

No Sarah. No nobody except
a girl in physics who talks to me,
but she talks to everybody.

Weeks 1 and 2 down and I skipped art
both weeks to avoid the hallway
where "it" happened.

Lots of ghosts, but no Devil.

Bus. Meat Palace.
Repeat.

THURSDAY, SEPTEMBER 13
Sometimes people put notes in my locker's grille

Sometimes one word, sometimes several,
never more than a sentence.

One at the end of last year said
sex isn't a hobby
and I had so many questions, the first
of which was
is putting weird notes in people's locker a hobby?

But that's the voice in my head
that says I'm too mature
to let these things bother me.

That voice is a little
overconfident.

Still, I had to laugh
when I looked up *hobby*

in the dictionary app
on my phone:

hobby: (n) an activity done regularly in one's leisure time for
    pleasure.

The note-leavers didn't waste any time this school year

so when I see the paper poking out from down
the hall, my stomach sinks, even as the mature
voice in my head says something tough
like *let's see if their handwriting has improved.*

It has.
Neat blue pen.
Circles dot i's.

But this one doesn't feel
like the others.

It says:

*What's done in the dark
will be revealed in the light*

and if I didn't know Sarah
was twelve miles away at her new
school, I'd think it was her
issuing one last barb—it sounds
just Bible-thumpy enough.

There are more words on the back
but I don't read them.

I may be a lot of things
but a masochist
isn't one of them.

FRIDAY, SEPTEMBER 14
I have two shirts for work and only ever wear one.

Terry is the new manager of the restaurant—transferred in when
    Joey got caught
setting up a fake robbery, emptying
the safe into the backseat of his car.

No bag or anything. Shit for brains.

But I would rather have Joey than Terry, who is older and goes to
    church and wears a tie
every day like he doesn't know this is a Meat Palace
in a nondescript part of town.

He lurks in drive-thru while I'm working, tells me to take my nose
    ring out.
He pretends he has to stand very close to me to see if I'm wearing it
    or not.
He thinks because I am sixteen that I don't know every trick in the
    book.

Maybe I don't. But I do know
there is a book

and that Terry pulls pages from it when he
    leans close to see my nose ring
    slips close behind me when he's restocking napkins
    stands close when the cashier steps out to take her break

13

Close close close

Never quite touching.
I know it will come—it always does
when men like Terry take your silence
for consent
or better yet
total
ignorance.

They know if you can claim not to know
that they can too,
like a hand down a teenager's bra
is just a mistake
a slip in a puddle
an agree to disagree.

I can hear my (ex) best friend's voice now, Sarah:
"If you hate it so much then quit."
"If it really bothers you then why haven't you said anything"

At the time (before she cut me off)
I didn't have the words that I have now.
I didn't know how to say

"This world is full of wolves. I've already
met worse wolves than Terry.
Terry is just a dog. Running from a dog

At this point,
at this juncture
in my career with wolves,

feels like admitting I'm a rabbit
when every day I feel more like a bull.

Sometimes wolves hunt bulls
and they win. But sometimes
they get the horns."

The first wolf I remember was bagging my mother's groceries.

I was fourteen and we'd just come from the pool.

(That doesn't mean I was wearing a bathing suit.
That doesn't mean I was wearing shorts.
People always wonder what I was wearing.
Why
when it comes to girls and wolves
do we let our brains look for reasons
why she deserved to be prey
before we notice his fangs?)

His name was Adam. He was twenty-one—
I learned this later.
At the time he was scanning my mother's
broccoli and bread
and when her eyes lowered to her purse
his rose to me.

Sometimes I remember the way the blush
felt crossing my cheeks and wonder
if I was to blame after all. After all
I was pleased to be noticed.
An older boy,
a man,
someone with perspective.

Not many people really noticed me at school
(before "it").

But Adam did.
I thought he saw something my peers
didn't see. I thought maybe in that moment
under the fluorescent lights
I had transformed into something worthy.

My father came back then from buying
a lottery ticket and if he saw Adam's eyes
he pretended not to.

My father never liked conflict.
He avoided it like chewed gum
on the sidewalk.

Maybe if he were different
everything else would be too.

You are the ghost in the ghost town when people pretend you are dead.

When I started sleeping with guys, my friendship with Sarah
    became an hourglass.
The first therapist my mother sent me to had one:
it gave me anxiety.
Watching the grains slipping through a hole I couldn't quite
    glimpse,
knowing that their transfer meant an end . . .
even though I looked forward to the end of every session,
I couldn't take my eyes from that hourglass.

Watching Sarah slip away was like that.
By the end, after hickeys
condom wrappers
pictures in my phone,
I could see the sand of her, sliding
down and away,
her calls and texts like the last few grains
slowing, slowing, gone.
Time's up.

She didn't know about the Colonel.
He was her favorite. He nominated
her for the national science fair.
He held her hand aloft when she won,
sharing the shining gold trophy,
the two of them posing for the photo
that would end up in the article online.

She didn't know. I didn't hold it against her.
She blinked at my questions when I asked
Is he ever weird
Does he give you a vibe?
Then, more directly, one night when
we were on her couch watching Netflix,
half-asleep:
Does he seem like a wolf to you

"No, Alicia. No. What the fuck Alicia"

After that I became strange to her, my skin
going translucent except for the part
on my neck where I let John Pogrund
suck a strawberry to the surface.

She saw that. Eventually, only that.
The girl she'd known since second grade
disappeared and Sarah didn't bother to look
for where she'd gone.

Sand and sand.
Time's up.
Time was always running out.

Sarah's speech

She begged me to come to church with her one week
even though I never really did church. I would spend
the night and go home in the morning while she put on
Easter-colored dresses and pantyhose.

It's okay, you can wear one of mine
when I begged off because of jeans
and maybe I should have smelled a trap,
but I put on the dress, I put on the shiny shoes

and I sat in youth group with Sarah on the day
everyone gave their prepared speeches
on topics of their choosing.

I don't remember everything Sarah said that day—
a three-minute speech is a lot to remember.
But I remember the last part very well
and even though she never looked in my direction
while she spoke, every word was aimed
at my skin, and lives there,
every vicious syllable:

I wear a purity ring so
  my mind remains innocent
  my body remains untouched
  my soul remains blameless
and when girls give in to flesh
they are none of those things
will never be those things
again.

It's not a story I tell.

Some people like talking about their firsts
but I don't. I'll say it here,
so that I say it somewhere.

It was Adam in a park after he'd persuaded
me to let him drive me home.

I had walked to Kroger to buy licorice
for the movies on Saturday.

I was crossing the parking lot when he pulled up,
still in uniform. Name tag still on.

I don't know what kind of car it was.
It was the kind that takes detours.

He said he wanted me to see his favorite
part of the park near my house.
I'd been there before. I'd been going
there since I was a little kid,
in the bleachers with Sarah, watching
her big brothers play T-ball.

He walked me through the woods
and he carried a blanket
and if I'm being honest I knew exactly
what he wanted and I never
told Sarah any of this because I knew
what she would say, even if she didn't say it out loud:

"You knew what he wanted to do
so why did you go?
You just walked beside him, like
a sheep to slaughter."

How do I say, I knew but wanted
to be wrong.
How do I say, I knew
and knew it was somehow
inevitable.
How do I say, a sheep
doesn't really know about
slaughter until their ears
are full of screaming.

But I didn't even scream.
It seemed ridiculous.
I was afraid someone on the T-ball field
would think I was dying, even
if a part of me
was.

My mother thinks I've dyed my hair red for attention—

How can I explain to her the ways that she is

right
and
wrong.

As of last night,
my hair is the color of a brick
the moment before it goes through
a stained-glass
window.

My hair is the color of a fire engine
driving through a burning building.

My hair is the color of a dart frog:
generations of death adapting
into this exact shade of poison.

It's called aposematism—
we learned about it in bio.
It's when an animal advertises
to predators that it is not worth
the attempt to consume.

Bright red and orange,
the colors of pain,
I WILL MAKE YOU SICK
I WILL KILL YOU FROM INSIDE YOUR THROAT

ATTENTION!
I MAY LOOK LIKE PREY
BUT I WILL END

YOUR
LIFE

My mother says I want attention
and maybe she's right
My mother says I am just making a statement
and maybe she's right

But in my mind it's not saying
please—
it's saying
don't

and this is how I know men
are not really wolves
because maybe
a wolf
would listen.

Another thought about Girls-Who-Do-Things-for-Attention

It's people's favorite way of dismissing girls
like me
or girls like
anybody:

"She's just doing it for attention"

Whether they're talking about
depression
or tattoos
or loud laughs

or sex
or rage

If a girl is doing any
of these things
she is "doing it for attention"

and I have
to ask

since when is that bad

and since when did people forget
that humans are like
flowers—
that we need
water and light
to grow?

MONDAY, SEPTEMBER 24
My life is leaving me behind and so is the bus.

We're already getting grades back and I give enough fucks to fill a
    thimble.
My fucks are the empty bulb of the hourglass:
I have none left, they have trickled down
like sand.

Still, when Ms. Gladstone asks for me to wait after last period, her
    eyes are honey brown
and the light in them shines sad,
and I think my mother might look like this
if she ever actually looked at my report cards anymore.

When someone who hates you tells you
you're falling behind
it has a way of turning your whole heart into a shield
to deflect the bullets of their words.
When someone who loves you tells you
you're falling behind,
the shield
    your whole life
turns to paper.

Ms. Gladstone talks to me
like she loves me, but when she asks
Is something going on
I still can't tell her because behind her
on the shelf is a picture of her
and the Colonel, hands linked—
Field Day, school colors painted on their faces,
smiles on their mouths. I tell her *nothing*
and that I have to catch the bus before
it leaves me behind too.

I sprint down the halls—
the bell has rung and no one can tell me
to stop, so I go and go, and if a child in me
survives, she imagines she is a horse in the Derby
and the other Thoroughbreds aren't even close.

Even so, the city bus leaves me, and to keep
running would be stupid, so eventually I stop,
my Meat Palace uniform dangling out of my backpack
like it too wishes it could escape
this day,
this life.

Coach Tinsley is walking toward the field
with the track team—he's new
this year—and he waves his clipboard,
shouts
"Come warm up. You'd smoke the girls at the Mason-Dixon" and I
    whisper
Fuck you
under my breath, under my breathless,
but for once I'm glad the intended ear can't hear
because the smile in his eyes is real
even if his offer isn't.

People who know you now vs. people who knew you then

Coach Tinsley is new this year and doesn't know
that I used to fly.
Coach Young retired and I'm glad,
otherwise she'd be at my locker asking me why the hell
I'm not running track this year. I don't think I could tell her.

I don't think I could tell her about the pair of shorts
crumpled in the bottom of my locker
like a corpse.

Tinsley seems nice enough but he doesn't know
that the girl he sees catching the bus
has two bloody stumps under her shirt
where wings used to be
and when he makes jokes about running

the stumps tingle, phantom limbs.

He doesn't know that he's talking to a ghost
that when he jokes about running

he's rubbing salt into a wound
he can't see.

Sometimes I pass people I used to run with—
we were never quite friends: the seniors I called close
all graduated—but I know they recognize me:
Jacob Wheeler
Tierra Pryor
Tabitha Renfro, eyes like diamonds
sharp and hard.
In her mind
who I am now
doesn't quite square
with the girl she ran 4x4 with,
but to look closer
would mean
just that: coming close,
and she's afraid
what I am
is infectious.

Thoughts before bed about the Devil.

I've never read the Bible: after Sarah
became a holy roller she was always trying to make me,
but after her speech, how could I?

Maybe I should read it, just to put things
in perspective.

Sometimes when I'm trying to talk myself out of
all the things that hurt me

I say to myself
"It's not even that big a deal."

A teacher at your school is an old
pervert.
So what if he _____
and _____
and _____.

Worse things happen:

the globe is heating
California is on fire
and people get murdered
and children go missing.

But if I agree with Sarah on anything
it's that the Devil might be all around us,
that maybe Evil has big projects,
like a history paper due at the end
of the semester, but It also has little
things It does throughout the day:

homework and busywork
and sewing projects, and maybe
the Colonel
is just a side hobby.

PS Devil

Because of her speech I know what Sarah's Bible says about lust
but even without the Book, I've learned that there are parts of me
    born in shadow.

Even when I'm not meaning to, I think of what Sarah said that day
under stained glass: *blameless.* And the equation seems so clear—

that if you welcome touch, you must also welcome blame,
and sometimes I can't make it make sense, but in my saddest
    moments all the pieces click:

that curious part of me born in shadow, that part that felt warm in
    fifth grade
when Samantha Westward's head dropped onto my shoulder while
    she slept on the bus;

the part of me that felt slick and shiny when Johnny Trejo
put me on his shoulders in the pool and spun me around until I
    screamed in the sun.

The existence of these parts meant I welcomed touch and therefore
    must accept blame.
By opening the door just that crack, just that inch, for Samantha,
    for Johnny, for the girl
I kissed at camp—
it was enough for Adam to squeeze in too.

But it doesn't matter anymore. Everything shiny and warm has
    burned off and I think I know
what the Bible says about lust and flesh, but what if there's no lust
    anymore—

just flesh,
methodical flesh?

What level
of hell
does that
doom me

to
and will it be
longer
than how
it feels
right now?

PPS Flesh

Over the summer I climbed into the backseat
of Ray Rangeland's Toyota
after he parked it by the river

and he seemed surprised when I took off my bra
but not more surprised than I was when he asked me
What's the rush?

We sat there so long that dew settled
on the grass
and on the hood of his car
everything sparkling.

He asked me when I feel the most free
and maybe it was because we'd been quiet so long
but I said
When I'm running.

We talked about the smell of grass
and Paramore
and how neither of our mothers could cook

and when he finally kissed my neck
I felt the dew on my own skin
all over. Behind my eyes.

After that he texted me for about a month
before he gave up.
That night by the river was the first
time since "it" happened
that I'd felt present in my body
for more than three minutes

and Ray might've understood
how running feels like freedom

but I don't think he could comprehend
how the flesh I wear is feral—

> that giving it kindness sends it farther
> into the trees, eyes glowing

> that it no longer understands softness
> when everything it touches turns to stone.

WEDNESDAY, SEPTEMBER 26
I am quiet.

My grandmother always said a watched pot
never boils,
but I am under too many eyes and still
constantly boiling
over.
The first time was Monday
with Mrs. Fisher.

Jack Driscoll
was sitting behind me, leaned close enough
for me to feel his breath on my neck.

He whispered something I couldn't hear but
I didn't need the words themselves to know the shape.

"Shut up," I whispered,
and then there were Mrs. Fisher's eyes,
magnified by her glasses,
magnified by disdain.
She was always telling me to put a sweater on.

On Monday I was already wearing a sweater
but I existed and my mouth was open
and the rifle of her gaze was
aimed at my chest.

"Be quiet" she said
And I said
"I am"
And she said it again
"Be quiet"
Like even my protest was an insult
And I said it again
"I am"
And she said "then why can I hear you"

And I said "maybe because you're listening
for me, you fucking bitch"

And beside me Chloe Wallis gasped
but that was the only sound until
the crackle of the walkie-talkie—
Mrs. Fisher calling security
"Escort Alicia to ISAP."

Rage is a chicken-or-the-egg scenario

I never used to feel this way:
the way rage pushes inside my body,
a red hand forcing
its way through my ribs and into
my chest, expanding like a sun.

I never used to get mad
about anything.

Maybe I didn't have anything real
to be mad about.

I don't know how to tend this garden
full of wild red things.

Before, I would have gone running. Now,
the things I do to stay calm are things
a stranger would do:

ride the bus
play card games on my phone: poker, spades, Razz
memorize street maps
play music so loud it makes my head hurt
    and never songs I like.

Anything to escape my brain, body.
Anything to be somewhere
    someone
else.

On the way to ISAP I pass memories:

The locker that used to be Sarah's,
where we were both standing when Jamie Waller
asked her to homecoming.

The stairwell where she snuck
a cigarette while I kept watch.

The doors to the auditorium
where she sang a Taylor Swift song
freshman year, before she gave it
all away for choir.

The cafeteria doors, where she pointed
at Blake Felipe and the other golden girls
and said "Those should be our people."

I pause at the locker long enough
to remember the Eleanor Roosevelt
quote Sarah pinned
on the inside:

Many people will walk in and out
of your life, but only true friends
will leave footprints in your heart

and I can't help but laugh
because footprints make it sound
like a crime scene,
and my whole life feels like it's wrapped
in that yellow tape.

While I walk the rest of the way to ISAP
I wonder if the quote is still in Sarah's locker

at her holy new school, if she ever looks
at her words and thinks about me.

But of course not
because a ghost doesn't
leave footprints.

In-school suspension is a paradise.

Mrs. Fisher sent me for the first time:
the perimeter of desks facing
the chipped beige walls.
No windows. One door.
Mr. West's desk at the head of the room
like a warden's roost.

I took my seat there among other people who
couldn't keep their mouth shut
couldn't keep their fists to themselves
couldn't keep from becoming
the shape of a thing that didn't fit
into a classroom made for compliance.

It wasn't so bad. Mr. West played
old music all day, half asleep,
enforcing nothing but near silence.
I sometimes snuck out my phone
to google the names of the singers:
Percy Sledge,
Tammi Terrell.

After my fourth visit to ISAP
I had learned some of the songs

by heart and that's when I met
Deja, both of us humming
"When a Man Loves a Woman."
Ms. McAllister sent Deja to ISAP
for wearing a weave that violated
the school handbook: a pink streak
at the front of her head.

Students must wear natural hair colors,
Deja mocked. *I guess they don't notice
you.*

I would argue that red is natural, I whispered.

She looked at my head, the color of poison.

For a fire engine, she whispered back, and we laughed
quiet enough so that Mr. West
stayed asleep. It was supposed to be
punishment
but it felt like swimming away from a shipwreck
and finding shore.
No eyes, no questions,
and above all
no Colonel.

I call him the Colonel because

everyone does.

When I entered Marshall as a freshman, blinking
like a cub leaving the cave,
I didn't know about the Halloween tradition:

all the teachers dressing up as
whatever their class voted they should be.

Ten years ago
maybe more
a student said he looked like
Colonel Sanders:
white hair
white mustache,
eyes twinkling under spectacles.

His hair has been white for a long time
I guess.

Every year the student body votes the same:
it's tradition now.

They line up and cast their ballots two weeks
before Halloween, everyone writing
THE COLONEL
in all their laughing penmanship.

I did too.
Until this year.
This year when I'm given my ballot
I write
WOLF
and drop it into the basket.

I know it will never be counted.
It will be pondered, dismissed.
He will never see it.

It's not the kind of action that matters
but I don't know what kind does.

My mother is missing jewelry and blames me.

We both know I'm a scapegoat. I entertain
her careful questions, the usual charade.

She asks me so she can feel that she has asked
someone.
My brother's door is closed. He's home
and not home.

He goes to another school, one with ROTC and a STEM program.
He liked ROTC until they made him cut his hair.
He liked STEM until he had to think.
He has new friends with long hair.
He has new friends who don't think.

Sometimes they come hang out in the basement
and my dad isn't here, and my mom is an adult
so she has to pretend that she's not
afraid of teenage boys

But they all smell like metal and never say hello and my brother
    never makes them
and things keep going missing.

One of them, Justin, is narrow and pale,
always smells like weed and cats.
He's the first person I've ever heard say
the N-word, dropped casually while
they play pool on the table my mother
no longer touches.

I look at my brother, alarmed,
and somewhere inside him is the way
we were raised, locked in a trunk,

and the trunk jumps at the sound of that
casual N, like a corpse trying to rise.

Justin sinks another stripe and my brother's
smile is a sailboat with a hole in its hull, limping carefully past
the floating corpse. I'm afraid of Justin staying in our house
but I think my brother is more afraid
of him leaving.

Text from a random at 9pm

Him: what are you doing
Alicia: nothing
Him: what would you rather be doing
Alicia: anything
Him: pick you up in 20?
Alicia: k

Sex is and isn't like the movies.

I have learned that there are different versions
of sex.

There's the kind where you kiss and there's the kind
where you don't.

There's the kind where you take off your socks and there's the kind
where you don't.

There's the kind you can tell people about and there's the kind
you can't.

Whenever I have sex it's the *don't* kind.
It's the *can't* kind.

I'm not sure when the transition happened.
It must have happened, the crossing of a line:
it must have been a fine one,
and maybe it's dotted in places, where girls
can weave into one lane
and then over into the other,
depending
on who
and when
they fuck
or who
or what
they are.

In the movies there are two kinds of women:

Ones who have sex and people still look them in the eye,
and ones who have sex and people look through them.

In the movies when women have sex they are often screaming.
I'd seen enough porn by the time
I was fourteen to know
that this is a script
we're all supposed to follow.

Over the summer I had sex with
Louis Knopp and he said I was
too quiet. He seemed
like the kind of guy who watches
a lot of porn. He was looking
right through me.

In the movies the camera can't go
inside the woman's head.

You never know if inside they are screaming
for a different reason.

tbh I don't really count Adam. I only count Renée.

We went to summer camp together when I was twelve.

We shared a cabin with five other girls, and when moonlight
would tiptoe through the cracks in the roof

Renée would tiptoe to my bed and crouch
there for hours, her face inches from mine, whispering

jokes into my hair, my laughter hidden by the green sheets
I'd brought from home. On the night before our parents

came to rescue us all from mosquito bites and sunburn
she crouched under our last moon together and kissed me.

I still remember the way she smelled like ferns
and something I couldn't place, something that smelled like
      home.

Sometimes I see a person and our whole lives unfold in my brain:

First date
First movie
First dessert
First kiss
First fight
First jealousy

Sometimes I see a stranger and imagine
what it would be like to hold their heart

alongside my own, protecting it
as my own. Sometimes I lock eyes
with a stranger, not when I'm playing
the Game but accidentally
across a crowded store
or sometimes on the bus

and I wonder if for a moment
in their head
we're married.

My whole head is hypothetical:
what if [this] happened
what if [that] hadn't

Sometimes I'm waiting for my mom
in the car outside the bank
and across the parking lot
glimpse my soul mate.

Sometimes it's a boy.
But almost always it's a girl.

SUNDAY, SEPTEMBER 30
My brother pretends he doesn't care.

On the rare evening we are in the same room at the same time
no one but us
I try to talk to him while he nukes pizza rolls.

How's school, David?
Any teachers you like
Any girls
Any boys, I might whisper.

I feel like a third parent
or a distant aunt
asking stale questions
to elicit any response
besides the stiff shrug.

He has eyes only
for pizza rolls.

Watching him in the kitchen
under the dim glare of three
bulbs, the rest burnt out and unreplaced,
I stare at his acne
the beginnings of a beard
the hollows under his eyes.

He's always been skinny but now
he looks like an opened envelope:
sharp corners and something removed
from inside, something important maybe—
not a bill but a certificate, a notice
that something critical has taken place
and I didn't get to it before
it headed for the shredder.

Sarah: Part 1 of (?)

Thinking about how if none of this had happened
we might still be friends.

Thinking about how if none of this had happened
I'd be on the school bus next to her.

Instead of here on the 22, unable to fall asleep
in case I miss the stop.

Thinking about how if none of this had happened
I could text her and tell her about David

About my parents
About the Colonel
About the Colonel
About the Colonel

But that's impossible because the Colonel
is where this all started. (Kind of.)

Thinking about how if none of this had happened,
none of this would have happened.

Sarah: Part 2 of (?)

Left on read for five months.
Sarah hasn't spoken to me, or even
answered a text, since May,
leaving the wound
of our friendship to fester
all summer.

Sometimes when I am walking home from
a boy's house or even
when a boy is unzipping my pants
I hear Sarah's voice close
in my ear like she is also in bed
on the couch
in the backseat
with me:

"You don't even like him.
If you don't like it why
do it?"

And even in my head I don't
have an answer other than
"At least I'm in control."

I know if I said it out loud
invisible Sarah's voice would say
"Control? Just play Xbox."
We used to play Halo
but like my mother's jewelry
the Xbox is one more
disappeared something,
like my dad, like my brother,
like my smile.

Sarah: Part 3 of 3

I've known Sarah since second grade and never told her
I like girls.

In fourth grade, I knew a girl named Frankie
who was always climbing trees
and she was the first Valentine I ever
cut out paper for instead of just using
the ones with cartoons you buy from Target.

I didn't write my name—even then I knew
that there were parts of me
that the light shouldn't
touch.

Celebrities announce they're gay

And it's hard even when you have millions of dollars
to insulate you from the weight of people's stares.

I don't even know if I'm calling myself gay.
I don't know anything
except
there is a list of things people
call me,
and so far
dyke isn't one.

TUESDAY, OCTOBER 2
Everything we're learning is supposed to matter

But with every class I sit through
trying to stare at the board and not
the inside of my head

it feels like a map to a land that doesn't exist.

Mrs. Fisher tries to make us see the shape of numbers
and the way formulas are like the world
but my world looks so different than the sterile
textbook examples.

Mr. Hudson lectures about history but ends up
talking about his divorce most days
tells us to go to law school so we don't get
screwed in the proceedings.

Mr. Mattson teaches physics and out of everything
this feels the most like something I can focus on

until he gets into gravity and I become hyper-
aware of the earth sucking me down
into the ground.

Only Ms. Gladstone's class feels like a refuge
because at least the worlds in the books she assigns
feel like me:

real and not.

People in pain
and telling
their story.

There's a new girl who flouts the uniform

in subtle ways. Bicycle shorts under her skirt,
black school tie instead of navy blue.
She has a nose ring

in her right nostril the size
of a pin's head. It's all the same
every day, like a uniform
she chose for herself.

She moves through the halls
like she's under water, slow
and graceful. When she passes

in the hallway, I almost
get caught in the
undertow.

Working drive-thru isn't all bad

especially when you're sharing the shift with someone
who hates people as much as you do.

Mariah taught me the word *misanthrope*
and while I have acquired my hate of people
Mariah says she was born this way. She
has a unique reason to hate every customer:

Her voice sounds like a car muffler.
He looks like he beats his kids.
He started his order with "gimme a . . ."

People with manners are occasionally spared, but she still hates
    them.

It has begun to rub off on me, and we have
contests for who can predict how ugly
the customer will be based on the sound
of their hungry voices through the speaker.

Cruelty feels like aloe on a sunburn.
After my fifth point in this game, predicting acne
and an overbite, I hear my grandmother's
voice in my head: *Keep making that face*
and it will stick like that.

I wonder if cruelty is the same,
a habit like any other, a muscle
flexed too often growing stronger
and stronger. But I can't make myself

Stop

Not until the voice I hear coming through
the speaker is one I recognize, and I wave
off Mariah's predictions.

The car pulls around.

Deja from ISAP, the streak in her hair blue
now. Her mother is driving, Deja
leaning across to pay.

She sees me, lights up, and her mother's
smile is like the door to a garden,
flowers beyond. I give them free
milkshakes and Deja gives me
her number.

Some misanthrope, Mariah says,
but even she is smiling,
and we let the cruel muscle rest
until the end of my shift.

Poems are like underwear.

Sometimes you want people to see them.
Sometimes they're uncomfortable.
Sometimes they're dirty, sometimes they're
full of blood.

Sometimes they're sticking out of your bag
and you drop them and someone picks them up that wasn't
supposed to and then they want to have a conversation about
your underwear that you weren't prepared to have.

Ms. Gladstone saw my poems, not my underwear.

She said if I ever want someone to read
them, she would like to see more.

I only ever write when I'm supposed to be
doing something else.

In class.
At work.
At home instead of homework.
On napkins, on receipts, not even a notebook.

I don't think what I'm writing about
is what Ms. Gladstone will want
to hear.

I don't know what other people's poems are about.
Shakespeare didn't write about the man on the bus
who pulled his junk out and waved it six inches from your face.
Robert Frost was writing about undisturbed snow, not
the smell of latex and locker room.
Not how, since you dyed your hair, random men call after you:
RED! on the street.
But you'd rather be Red than Alicia.

It's not always men.

There's a girl named Lisa who never
remembers my name but always wants
to give me a hug. It feels like middle school

when everyone wants to hug everyone—
the churn of energy and hormones
makes you grabby and strange.

Lisa is grabby and strange. She always
calls me the wrong name, always wants a hug
in the hallways between classes,
always holds me a little too tight.

There's an urgency, a rawness
when she clutches her arms behind
my back that makes me think
she could possibly be a wolf
or maybe has just been bitten by one
already.

Sometimes I feel like a narcissist

for thinking people are watching me
but when there are slips of white paper
stuck into my locker, I know it can't
all be in my head.

I throw them away without reading them.
The paper itself makes me feel hunted.
I don't need any more reasons
for my heart to pound
when walking down certain hallways
is enough.

In the back of my mind is the mature voice

quiet and cautious:

You could tell Ms. Gladstone about the notes.
You could tell her you feel

like a rabbit
    on the run

like a ship
   filled with holes

Maybe the notes in your locker
could be bread crumbs
she could follow to the center
of your heart, where the real
problems are.

Hey, mature voice,
it must be nice to think
things are that simple,

to think things can be separated
so neatly,

to think that pulling one thread
won't unravel the whole sweater.

I may not know everything, but
I know enough to be sure
that every secret in my life
is connected at the core—

I don't know what the notes mean
or who's writing them, but
I do know that shining a light
means you see what's in the dark

and a girl can only handle
so many monsters, especially
when there's one staring back
in the mirror.

What my brother and I used to be:

Before I grew boobs and he grew tall
people would ask if we were twins.
We're not. The things
that made us the same
were the trappings of childhood:
big teeth, the same haircut
because I always wanted
to be like him
and our mom
didn't care to differentiate
daughter from son. She loved
us the same and so if we looked
the same
it was a reflection of her heart.

Middle school came and we split off,
a thread fraying as it made its way
through the needle, pieces of him
going that way and pieces of me
somewhere else.

Maybe that's just the way it is.

Maybe I watch too many movies:

the big brother swooping in
to protect her, or at least leaning
in the doorway of her room,
distant but warm.

My brother and I used to be something
resembling close.
Maybe the way it is

is the way it always was
and I was too much of a kid
to notice.

"Since Sarah left me"

Sounds like a marriage breaking apart,
a wife writing poems about her husband
going off to war. That's a little
what it feels like when I think about Sarah
even if her war is a private one,
the battle against sin. She goes

to the big fancy Christian school now
and I remember somehow knowing
even as a fourth grader
when she joined youth group
at her church,
that her going would change things.
I just didn't know how much—

how virginity would become a coin in her purse
how hell would become a comet in her palm
how judgment would become a sword in her belt.

Since Sarah left me
means "since she went to that school."
Since Sarah left me
means "since she stopped answering my texts."
Since Sarah left me
means "the day she left me standing at the bus stop alone."
Since Sarah left me
is many events rolled into one wound that wears my best friend's face.

Wolves love bus stops.

I remember exactly what I was wearing
the first time I took the bus alone.

High-waisted jeans, a T-shirt that showed an inch of my stomach.

I'm always thinking about
what I was wearing when.

Standing by the telephone pole that day,
staring at my phone,
I transformed without knowing.

Girl into rabbit, soft furred thing with belly
exposed, ripe for fangs.

Eyes became teeth. Men in cars rolling past with
no rules, no accountability, half-domesticated

Howling out their windows, HEY BABYing with their wives on
    mute, NICE TITS to the beat of
stereo music. WANNA FUCK when it's more than one in the car
    and they're

entertaining/impressing/masturbating
each other with my embarrassment.

Although I wasn't embarrassed at first.
When you're fourteen and just realizing
maybe someone thinks you're beautiful
you can mistake the sound of howling
for a heart song.

It's never a heart song.

I thought I was receiving compliments
at the bus stop. I thought it was about me
but
it's about them:
how something about a girl alone
at a bus stop makes their fangs grow past their lips
and the gathering feeling of saliva makes them want to spit these
     words into the sky.

That was two years ago.
I'm used to it now.
When I told this story to Sarah
she said *you were fourteen*
why were you showing your stomach
walking around by yourself?

The Game I play that I never lose/win.

Sometimes I take my break at Taco Bell
across the street. We get free
food working at Meat Palace (when the manager is out.
So more like: we *take* free food)
but eventually your entire life starts to smell
like beef and I sometimes take refuge
in the smell of beans instead, a refugee
in another fast-food land.

I sit at a corner table scribbling on a napkin
and nearby a man sits alone, finishing
his lunch. He's wearing a uniform but I don't
know what kind. Medical maybe. Ambulance
driver. EMS. I don't know. It doesn't matter.

I see him because he sees me.

He's looking at my legs under the high table
where I perch. Khakis stretched tight
while I'm sitting down, my thighs flattening
and spreading.

He doesn't try to hide that he's looking.
We make eye contact.
He's probably twenty-five.

The Game I play doesn't have rules.
Sometimes I don't know I'm playing it.

I am sixteen and what Adam called jailbait.

This Game means I make myself bait. I stare
at the man too old to be staring back
and wait for him to notice I'm sixteen
wait for him to care
wait for him to recognize what should be a deal breaker.

He stands to clear his tray and I wonder
briefly if he's leaving. My stomach flares
with disappointment
with relief
but then he's coming over, eyes narrowed,
mouth curling in a smile, and all I think is

There you are.

He asks my name and I tell him.
He asks if I work here. I point across the street.
He teases me: something about *do I like beef.*

I've heard that one before.

I ask how old he is and he says twenty-seven.
He asks for my number.
He doesn't ask how old I am.
When I give him my number he looks me in my eyes and tells me
    he'll call me later.

I wonder how long I'll play this Game: testing men
for fortitude
wondering when adults will be adults.
He leaves with my number.
I finish my tacos.

I have done this so many times,
always winning,
winning myself
into oblivion.

I never try with women.
I know it wouldn't
work.

Sometimes it settles in later:

I have given a twenty-seven-year-old man my phone number.
The reality rattles in my ribs.
I always hope they won't call:

Prove me wrong.
Prove me wrong.
Prove me wrong.

They always call.
They think they have found something easy.
They never guess that I'm thinking
So have I.

My life and school are overlapping universes.

Sometimes when I walk the halls, class to class,
I feel like I am more than a Martian.

Mars is too close.

Outside these walls, I am something stranger than my peers,
who laugh with teeth and eat school lunch
and do their homework and can make their mouths
say *yes ma'am* to a teacher who doesn't hate them.

My orbit crosses this place, and so I go.
My planet has no sun, no moon, I don't know
what I'm even orbiting. I'm not a planet
at all, just a lonely asteroid
hurtling through space.

But then there's the new girl.
I learn her name is Geneva.

She still wears black every day and
today when I pass her in the hall
I'm studying her as if with a telescope
and her eyes lift and catch mine.
Her black lips crack to
release a sliver of a smile
and without meaning to
I think
Oh, there's the sun

Envy is a sin too, I think,

and I almost
almost
text Sarah to say "look how
I know all the things that turn the soul
into a rotten apple"
but I think if my soul is an apple, Sarah
has already condemned it to a ditch
or maybe the mouth of a dead pig.

There is a girl I envy at school—lots
of them if I'm being honest: the easy
way they move through life, how
the hallways are just another red carpet.

But if envy is an apple
(to continue the fruit metaphor)
Blake is the core.

She has red hair
    —naturally red: not like mine—
not the color of poison
but the color of new pennies shining
at the bottom of a wishing well.
She is the wish in human form.

Blake is a senior and she plays field hockey.
Blake wears the right amount of makeup.
Blake has had the same boyfriend
since freshman year, which is something like
a sign of her purity
a testament to her goodness.

Blake's hair is always moving and her smile
is always glinting and she is quiet but not
too quiet.
She is funny but not a ham.

She wins field hockey games but never showboats.

How do I put it into words?
Blake is a new penny.
Blake is a wish.
Blake is who I wish I could be.

Blake's friends, however,

have the same white teeth as Blake
but they might as well be sharpened
into points.

Last year I was a different kind of creature
to them—the kind that drifted
by unseen and unthreatening: track team   ponytail   no makeup

and the only thing that has changed
besides everything
is the track team.

But rumors are faster
than I am
    (was)
and when they see me in the halls
I realize that to me
    I am a ghost
but to them
    I am a monster,

that like Frankenstein
I have stepped outside of some sacred
agreement, except I'm not
the mad scientist
but rather
the thing rising from the table

and when I pass too close to Blake's
friends, their eyes
are torches, lunch utensils
are pitchforks.

In their minds there are two kinds
of women, and only one
is allowed to be human

so they spend all their time
making sure everyone knows
exactly which one
they are, and that means
making sure I know
exactly which one
I am.

I cut art again

because I just can't bring myself
to walk down that hall, knowing
what I'll have to pass to get there.

So I wander the school
empty and echoing
like the Colosseum
until I dodge into the auditorium

to avoid security and find
one of Mr. Hudson's classes
onstage, two microphones
like bookends, Deja
at one and Clay Bevin
at the other, while the rest
of the class takes up the first two rows,
watching.

Clay is finishing his side of the debate
but hearing his closing remarks
is enough: *and that's why cancel*
culture is un-American, because
if we can't separate the art
from the artist, then we foster
a culture of victimhood

and everyone down front claps,
a couple whoops before Deja
starts to speak:
Victimhood *is a funny word.*
You talked for ten minutes but still
didn't give an example of what being "canceled"
has cost anyone besides hurt feelings.
All the people you named are still rich
Are still famous
Are still free
Are still racist or hateful
Still have the benefit of their good name
so what the hell has cancel culture
actually cost them?

And Mr. Hudson interrupts, calling
Foul language is automatic forfeiture!

and no one in the rows of seats claps for Deja
and she looks so alone up there
on her side of the stage
the new red streak in her hair like a spark
from my own head

so I stand up and applaud as loud as I can
screaming until my throat sandpapers
until everyone in her class turns around
in their seats, shocked
until I see Deja's smile light up the stage
until Mr. Hudson chases me out
right into the security guard's waiting frown.

And then
it's back to ISAP.
But it was worth it.

First text from Deja

Deja: Why do you work at Meat Palace?

Alicia: Because I need money

Deja: But why Meat Palace tho? Why beef

Alicia: It was that or Taco Bell

Deja: I feel like Taco Bell would've been a better fit

Alicia: why?

Deja: bc you're kinda spicy

Alicia: it's fake

Deja: so's Taco Bell 😊

Alicia: lol fair

I visit my dad's new apartment.

He thinks it's temporary.
I can tell by the way he only unpacks
what he thinks he needs—
boxes lining the walls
as if in waiting.

My mother has kicked him out before.
But this was the first time
she had proof: iMessages
he deleted from his phone
but not his computer.

Rookie, even now.

He wants me to spend the night
wants to talk about my brother
wants to talk about fixing
our family.

Somehow when he envisions all the things
that need fixing, all the things
that are wrong with our lives
in a gallery of portraits
and fractured landscapes

he never sees himself
in the frame.

One thing I never do

is send anyone photos of my face.

I've never understood the way other people
can take selfies so effortlessly.

In the mirror I am pretty:
my eyes look normal, nice lashes
my skin is okay.
My hair has always been kind of nice
without much effort.

But in the eye of my iPhone
I become something by Picasso,
nose like a book that has not been properly shelved
eyes blank

I look hollowed out
and pale, the way a mannequin
might look if suddenly
realizing it had thoughts
but unable to think about anything
but plastic.

When guys ask for pictures
I just send a photo of my boobs
because even though everyone
is always staring at them
they don't have eyes,
and with no head
who could ever really say
whose chest

whose mole
whose skin with heart beneath
the photo really contains?

I look for the new girl's Instagram

All I have
is her first name
and I know
it's not enough
but I look
anyway
almost afraid
to find her,
the phone
close to
my face
in the
    dark.

Deja invites me to the mall

and neither of us have any money
not really
but we walk around and look at things
we might buy if we did,
and Deja tells me about how the concept of the mall
is going extinct
that everyone shops online and that all these big cavernous
buildings full of things no one needs
should just be converted into parks.

Public space, she says,
and I feel like I've entered
a conversation with a college professor
who just happens to look like a teenager in Nikes.

She wants to major in business economics.
I don't know what that means.

The mall feels empty and when I say so she asks me
if I know why.

   No.
Because last year they banned unaccompanied minors from shopping.
   It's code for Black teenagers. They think we steal. And now their
   stores are shutting down. Bird-brained.

I think of me and Sarah
and how many pairs of earrings
we lifted every weekend,
how many stupid things like socks
like keychains
like makeup.

(Stealing must not have registered
the way sex did
in Sarah's hierarchy of sins.
Ditto smoking.)

Deja smiles at me over the top
of one of those racks of jewelry
that spin.

The only reason they haven't kicked my ass out is because I'm with you.
How does it feel, for your whiteness to be a shelter,
a chaperone?

And I'd never thought about being white like that—
as a possession, as currency—
but I shrug and say
Do you want me to steal you some earrings?
and Deja laughs and laughs and laughs.

Sometimes, only sometimes,

I feel mad about being white
and all the things I'm not supposed to think
or say. My life feels like a minefield already:
I have big breasts and a big mouth
and I'm supposed to hide them both,
and sometimes
only sometimes
white feels like just one more thing
I have to hate
about myself.
And then I watch videos while waiting for the bus home
and I see
the never-ending pale parade
the advertisements for beauty products
    that define *me* as Beauty
the way people
    who look like me
are always stealing ideas from girls
    who look like Deja
how when a girl with my face goes missing
    voices all rise in one unified horror.
And then I'm still mad, but not at the people
who call all this white shit what it is,
but at myself—and the magician—

for almost falling for
a trick as obvious as a coin
disappearing behind the curve of a
   very
        Caucasian
          ear.

There's something hidden there that I'm not smart enough to see

but it makes me think of my brother's friend Justin
and the way he smirks when he says the N-word—
like it puts money in his pocket
like it puts helium in his balloon—
and I think there must be something we have in common
besides simply being white
that makes me hear *white* and cringe
that makes him hear *white* and grin

because they are opposite reactions,
but opposites are related *because* they're opposites

so what force is pushing on me
and Justin both
and why does it feel like the same
tug-of-war
between the Pure Girl
and the Whore?
When my knee jerks against *white*
and I defend myself against a sword
that doesn't exist

who is blowing up my balloon?
What pennies drop into my purse?

69

When I get home, my brother asks me where I've been

and I should be happy to hear his voice, speaking
unprompted, but his tone is vinegar
and sours the whole room.
So instead of answering,
I ask why the fuck he cares
and he just stares at me across
the kitchen like the distance
between us is a canyon
with no bridge, and also
like he's seen inside my phone
and my head.

Justin told me he heard you're a dyke.
Are you a dyke?

It drains the poison from my eyes,
and poison was the only thing
I had. The one thing I haven't
been called has spun itself
into existence, and in a way
I'm not even that angry
because, of all the things
they say about me
    (*they*—the mysterious, faceless *they*)
this one feels more personal,
like whoever hurls this insult
has looked at me and
for once
seen something true.
In the end, I say nothing

and he leaves
and his doorway becomes
another place I cannot cross
without judgment.

My brother taught me to read

but not sitting by my side and trailing his fingers
across the words on the page, or sounding out
a single syllable.

He's eighteen months older, and learned to read first.
He would sit in the car on the way to church
when we still went
and read all the billboards out loud:

> Save 10% on your car insurance with GEICO
> Lion's Den Palace for Men
> Buy one get one free at Kroger

I envied the way his eyes translated the mysteries all around me
and I raced to catch up.

He was given a book of poetry when we were little.
He wasn't into it
and so it fell into my hands.

I've been scribbling ever since
never in a notebook because it feels
presumptuous,
feels like I'm calling myself something
other than the obvious: GIRL WITH THOUGHTS
SHE SOMETIMES WRITES DOWN.

I used to write my brother notes.
When we were ten and twelvish
we would slip paper under each other's doors
at bedtime and in the morning swap answers
before school.

When he turned thirteen the answers turned
into those grains of sand at the end of the hourglass:
slower, trickling.

There had to have been a last note.
I wouldn't have recognized it at the time
not knowing it was the last.
You never know if something is the last
until it is.

Sometimes I want to try again and ask him more questions:
Where do *you* go at night
Where is the Xbox
Why are you friends with Justin
What do you think is going to happen to us

But his light is never on
and my fingers can't quite force themselves
to spell out his name.

MONDAY, OCTOBER 22
I saw the Colonel today

for the first time this year, successfully
tunneling through the school the way I have
like a mole.

He didn't see me.
That's it. That's the poem.

The saddest part about the Colonel

(Well, not the saddest part)
is that he was never part of the Game
where I meet a man's eyes
and wait for him to be an adult.

He's the one who put me on the board,
shoved dice into my hand.

With the Colonel I walked into his classroom
hating science, but wooed by the way he made
everything a joke, always teasing, *the cool teacher*.
He did it with everyone, not just girls like me—
baby fat migrating up toward bras—
had the same imp smile for every student.

When I looked in his eyes
when I stayed after class to ask questions
it was because he made me feel safe
enough to admit I never really understood
basic things like balancing equations
or naming and formulas

I came to him as a student
and he came to me as a teacher
until
the day
he came to me
as a wolf.

That's when the Game began.

Maybe not right away.
His arm around my shoulders
his fingers at the edge of my bra,
it pulled all my atoms apart
then dropped them into stasis.

Weeks passed
and months,
everything that made me
who I am
rearranged,
like Dr. Manhattan in the test chamber
put back together as something
not quite human.

I saw on Tumblr that people with trauma
will sometimes reexpose themselves to trauma
over and over until they think they understand what happened.

I don't know why I play the Game.
I understand what happened.

My biology teacher hurt me
and if I was smarter I could find a clever metaphor
about chemistry that tells why and how
but the simplest way to say it is that
I was a student but he saw a rabbit
and no one will believe me
because he's the most
beloved wolf in school.

Afterthought about wolves and their prey.

I try not to say *sheep*.

In fairy tales, wolves are after sheep,
and maybe it's because Grimm and Mother Goose
and all that old European bullshit
always had wolves and sheep on the brain.

But in *this* country wolves hunt
deer
elk
rabbits

Everyone thinks sheep are stupid.
Maybe they are—I've never met one.
I know they're supposed to do what they're told.
They follow the herd.
They walk willingly to the butcher,
or so the butcher says.

When we say "wolf in sheep's clothing"
it's a comment about the wolf
but also about the nature of sheep,
easily fooled.

I have never been a sheep
in that way.
But wolves hunt me anyway.

I fell asleep in Algebra II.

When people talk about the best dreams
they always talk about flying,
their arms becoming wings that bear them
into the sky.

I never dream about flying.

In my best dreams
I am running.

I'm running so fast
the ground ceases
to exist, I become one
with the wind.

My feet carry me to something
that feels like sky.

Maybe that's the same thing
as flying.

The new girl passed my locker today.

Geneva.
I should call her by her name.
But *the new girl* still feels right
because she is the only thing
that has felt new in a long, long time.

In bed thinking of sins

I wasn't raised to think about sins, deadly or otherwise.

I wasn't raised to wonder if I was going to heaven or hell.

Sarah put these thoughts in my head.
So did the whole world, I guess.

We're always so preoccupied
with what happens when we die.
We don't even know
what's happening while we're alive—

our world swarms with secrets and we walk down aisles of them
like Walmart purgatory.

I wonder if Geneva goes to church or if
like me
she's looking for salvation
elsewhere.

My brother got home at 1am on a school night

and my mother didn't even ask him
where he'd been. She asked for his car keys
and he didn't give them to her
and she couldn't make him
and my dad's not here
to help.

My brother's name is David.

I have to remind myself
because it doesn't fit him
anymore.
David seems like a gentle name
or at least it always has to me.

Since he started hanging out with Justin
and Scotty
and Andrew

his edges all seem harder,
even without the ROTC cut.

I stand at the kitchen counter with my mother
when they all come in from having been
somewhere
and we watch silently
as they all troop past
saying nothing
not even hello
and file down to the basement
to play pool on the table
my mother paid for.

When we hear the door shut my mother
breathes out
like she's cooling coffee
and says "where does he meet all this white
trash" and my mind says what I've heard
Deja say:

*White is white
and modifying* trash *with* white

implies that trash
is Black by default

or maybe
trash *is modifying* white?

but my mouth says
"I don't know"

because trash or not
I don't know where my brother meets boys
whose smiles look like razor blades
dragged across skin
when we were raised to never
draw blood.

Deja texts me to say that ISAP stands for In-School Adjustment Program

and we LOL over all the things we've adjusted in that quiet gray
    room:

Deja: my bra
Alicia: my posture
Deja: my stance on teachers' pensions
Alicia: the height of Mr. West's chair when he was in the bathroom
Deja: my circadian rhythm
Alicia: what??
Deja: SLEEP
Alicia: my need for light and air
Deja: anything but my attitude
Alicia: never that

I almost text her to ask if she ever had class with the Colonel,

but decide not to because there's no way
if she says *yes* that I can keep from asking
about wolves
and she may not even believe in them.

Whatever creature she thinks
I am,

she has decided to talk to me anyway
and I don't want to test
limits that surely exist.

Wolf is an apt metaphor because

* sometimes they hunt in packs
* a werewolf can make more werewolves with its bite

I can't think of anything else.

I kind of like
actual wolves.

They're endangered.
I wish these were.

Sometimes I'm torn about eyes

because there are times when I'm
riding the bus
walking to class
shopping with my mom,

when I will look up to find
eyes on my body,
hungry stare, sometimes someone
my age and sometimes
not, a stare that turns me
into a meal.

And sometimes I like the way it feels
like someone has lit a torch
in my stomach in deepest night
and all the moths come seeking.

Is it possible
to like something sometimes
and hate it other times?

Am I allowed
to decide when
I want to be
a feast?

I should be doing homework

but I can hear my brother and his cadre
of losers, shouts and laughter rising
through the floor. I am conscious then
of what is below me and it makes me think
of what is above me, and when I think
of what is above me, I think

of Blake Felipe.

I'm not obsessed with her—if I'm obsessed
with anything, it's the architecture of a Good Girl—

and I cruise her Instagram
studying the way her boyfriend laces his fingers

around her belly, the way her smile is the same
in photo after photo, like every day is ctrl + c
    ctrl + p-erfect.

Her hands clasp his and she wears a ring
like Sarah's and I wonder if she prays

if she carries heaven in her pocket, and if
she ever slips the silver over her knuckle

and her underwear down over her knees,
taking everything off, even the plaster smile.

I wonder if she ever touches herself in the dark,
if she's ever cheated on her four-year boyfriend

just to see, just to taste another person's sweat,
to watch her lucky-penny hair sweep over their chest.

I know she has not. These are all the ways we are different.
These are all the ways that she is gold and I am rust.

And I could blame the Colonel—and for some things, I do—
but when my phone's screen goes to sleep I think again

of the doorway I inched open, the box whose lid I cracked,
how everything that slithers through is my doing.
In the dark my breath hisses like a serpent.

FRIDAY, OCTOBER 26
Today I made myself go to art

and when I passed his classroom
it was different.

82

The door was closed.
I can only remember it
being closed
one time—the first time.
I was in it.

I couldn't breathe.

I froze on the way to studio,
everything in me turning heavy—
the hallway is a river
between classes, rushing and rushing,
and around me people pushed.

I was a blockade at the center, a dam
of still flesh, staring at the closed door,
its empty window. I couldn't make myself
move closer, but my neck strained
my eyes trying to become X-rays

Was someone inside
Was someone inside
Was someone inside

Don't you have somewhere to be?

Ms. Balwick, staring me down with those eyes
teachers get when they have already heard
that you're a problem,
when they're waiting for you to be that problem
so they can solve you right over to ISAP.

I say nothing, make my body unfreeze,
walk toward studio one heavy step at a time

and the hallway rushes around me but behind me
the door
stays
closed.

His door is always open.

That always-open door is part of his mythology:
he always wants to be bothered.

Even when he's grading he will always smile
at an interruption. That smile zeroes
in on you until the rest of the world fades
and you feel important
seen
heard.

Sometimes I walk past that always-open
door and the always-open
wound it rubs raw by sight alone
throbs.

I see the skeletons along the back wall
some human
some not
studies of anatomy
the nervous system,
circulatory,
and though the Colonel
isn't a killer
whenever I pass, I can't help but wonder
how many other bodies

he has on display
in his mind.
But today the door was closed.
And I can't stop thinking
about why.

Geneva/the new girl is good at art.

She doesn't mind when paint gets all over her.
I wash my brushes twice at the sink
for an excuse to pass by,
peek at her portrait—a woman's smiling face—

but mostly to glimpse her hands

the way her brown skin looks like Earth itself
splattered in blue and green
like I am flying high above the clouds
and looking out the window of my lonely ship
to see her,
the planet,
waiting.

It's more than halfway through October.

The Halloween contest is approaching,
when all of us will gather in the cafeteria
the tables folded away.

I've seen this show twice now:
clapping and shouting
before I knew better.

The Colonel will perform:
white suit, cane, and grin.

The cool teacher,
the funny guy,
the one who lets you get away
with everything
never writes a detention
except once when Vic Parrent
punched a guy during bio.

The good guy, the smile
and twinkling eyes
are both reputation and résumé.

I plan my sick day now.

I should know the date of the first time "it" happened, but I don't.

It was spring—months after Halloween.

That's all I remember.
Before then I had sat in his classroom
learning to trust my scientific abilities,
and by the time the Halloween contest
rolled around I was already an acolyte:
I had written COLONEL SANDERS
on the paper just like everyone else,
shoving it into the ballot box
while we all laughed, knowing.

He stayed after school sometimes.
So did I, for track.

I popped my head in to say hi,
entered when he motioned me inside.

I was wearing school-issued blue shorts.
There was a falcon on my chest.

He smiled and closed the door.

Deja always brings her food—

and sometimes as I'm leaving the cafeteria
her lunch block comes in, and I overhear
her friends teasing her for the woven bag
she carries, the Post-it note that her mother
writes with a heart fluttering to the tabletop.

Sometimes she sees me watching
and beckons me over, but
I always say no, point to the door
like I have somewhere urgent to be.

She always smiles like she understands
even if she doesn't, and her friends
raise eyebrows,
but she never stops asking.

TUESDAY, OCTOBER 30
Greetings from the pit in my stomach.

This day has been lurking on the horizon
like a distant hurricane
threatening the coast where my heart
has made its home.

It's 1:30pm and I'm sitting in Mrs. Fisher's class.
Her phone rings, the mostly ignored thing that sits on her desk.
She answers it, and I already know even before her eyes
travel across the classroom to my face.

Yes, she is, she says. And *Yes, I will.*

She hangs up.

Alicia, she says. *The Colonel would like to see you in his class.*

And she doesn't bat an eye, and neither does anyone else.
Why would they?
He is a well-hidden wolf.

When I don't move, she blinks, stares

Did you hear me?

In the hallway, the air
sticks in my lungs like tar.

I pass an emergency exit and something inside me considers
lunging through, triggering the alarm
that will make the ceilings rain and send
my peers out into the first cold day of fall.

But Principal Warren is there and asking if I have a hall pass
and I don't, but I tell him the Colonel sent for me
and all he says is
Well, don't keep him waiting.

His classroom smells the way it always has.

He asks me to sit at his desk and grade freshman papers.
I say nothing.
Just take the red pen

mark everything wrong.

I should be in Mrs. Fisher's class failing
Algebra II
but I'm here
and he's here
and his classroom door is closed

and maybe I'm supposed to write
about what happens next
but maybe if I pretend
none of this is real
it won't be.

When I leave his class I feel like the jack-o'-lanterns

they have decorating the front of the school.
Hollowed out, eyes like wounds.

I go back to Mrs. Fisher's class
and all I can think about is what Sarah
would say:

There you go, lamb
to slaughter, you knew why he called
you to his class, you knew when
he started to close the door
but you still sat there quiet

so that must mean you wanted
to be there, that some part of you
likes it, likes him. You already
sleep with everyone else,
why is this any different?

And her voice in my head
is so loud that it drives me
to the bathroom to puke until
like a jack-o'-lantern
everything inside
is scraped out
and my teeth are slick
with slime.

The text I don't send Sarah

Remember that time in fifth grade when we went to the Halloween
    dance dressed as bats but Mr. Andrews thought we were devils
    and said we couldn't come in and we called your mom crying?
    Every day feels like that.

Hey Sarah, do you think I'm a monster? Do you think I'm a dyke?
    Do you think I'm a devil?

Do you?

The thing about giving things away

is that people think
because you give things
away

that means
nothing
can be taken
from you
even if the thing
you give away
is your body.

Is that what
it means
to be canceled?

Is canceled
like math:
giving
and
taking away
canceling each other out
until
nothing
          of me

is
left?

WEDNESDAY, OCTOBER 31
Halloween

I tell my mom I'm sick.
I can't bear to go to school
and see the Colonel
in his white suit, square-fanged,

while around me
Geneva and Deja
and everyone else
clap and cheer
for a wolf
dancing onstage.

MONDAY, NOVEMBER 5
The only thing I can paint in studio is red.

Not a red apple
Not a red rose
Not a red anything
just my brush dragging slow
and deadly across the canvas
like stripes of exposed organs
like roadkill
like a vein opening for a knife.

Ms. Gupta pauses at my shoulder
and I can hear the wet sound
of her mouth starting to open
and then changing its mind
before she moves on
down the aisle, away
from the scene of this murder.

My hand keeps moving
and so does the clock's
and by the end of the period
I am just standing to yank
the whole painting into the trash

when someone appears at my side
close enough for me to smell
their lotion: rose water,
sweet and soapy.

I look up and find Geneva's eyes
studying the riot on the page
the canvas white only at the edges.

I don't know what it means is all I can manage,
because this is what Ms. Gupta is always asking
us to consider, but

Geneva only cocks her head, and I get the feeling
she's walking through the mess of it,
seeing that some of the organs exposed
on the page
are mine.

I don't think you have to, she says.
Not until you're ready.

Thank god we still have a house phone

because when I get home from school
before my mother
I see we have a voicemail.

I expect telemarketing
a dentist appointment reminder
but Ms. Benton, the dean of eleventh grade,
is speaking into our kitchen
telling "the parents of Alicia Rivers"

that
"your daughter"

has been having
"some problems"
at school

and she would
"love to speak to you"

about "finding a solution"
to this "erratic behavior."

I press delete before she can say goodbye,
and tell myself it's not wrong
because the message was for "the parents
of Alicia Rivers," plural,
and only one of them
lives here.

Text from a random who is less random because he goes to my school

Him: Me and Travis want to see you

Alicia: "See" me

Him: lol don't act like you haven't done two guys before

Alicia: I don't have to act

Him: are you coming over or not?

Him: Travis knows you're wild, it's fine

Alicia: I have a paper due tomorrow

Him: I didn't know hoes did homework

Travis is on the football team and likes to hit people

I have felt afraid many times
    when getting into a car
    when stepping inside a house
    when walking down the hall at school

but this fear is different.

It's the same feeling of standing too close
to a railroad track,
the train rushing past in a blur of metal
and noise

or teetering at the edge of a bridge
with no rail, nothing but space,
emptier even than me.

No, I don't think Travis would kill me.
Nothing that dramatic. It's just
that they don't even pretend
to like me—for them, the insult
is part of the fun.

This fear is like watercolor—
to these two boys I am already half-
invisible. They are the water:

under their existence
I feel myself fading, spreading thin
until there's only a ghost
of a ghost
left.

ISAP for skipping art class again

and Deja isn't there, so I just sit and stare at the ceiling,
tapping my foot to the song I now know is
"If You Think You're Lonely Now" by Bobby Womack.
ISAP is good for one thing—I could probably go on a game show now
a game show for only old music
and clean up. Win a car
that I could drive offstage
and toward the horizon.

Mr. West dozes in his chair and between card games
on my phone, I stare at his round stomach,
rising and falling, Bobby Womack near his ear.
I wonder if ISAP for him
is like a chamber for time travel,
where he falls asleep
and the music transports him to when these songs
were the soundtrack to his life.

I have songs like that. Some old, like I absorbed
them through my parents, and some not.
Billie Eilish has a song called "Bad Guy"
and even though it's not new
it still calls up something familiar in my skin
that makes it timeless.

Bad guy
the equivalent of a viper
in a dress.

I don't wear dresses. But sometimes
when I'm trying to transform myself
into someone with a heart made of iron

I tell myself this is what I am,
that my hair is red like a siren
and not a salamander

that I am a vicious man-eater
and not a rabbit

not a rabbit
not a rabbit
not something so easily consumed.

I am the thing with the fangs.
Not a wolf but something more monstrous,
not a sad girl with a scar across her soul
but a creature who eats souls
for breakfast.

I see it when I finally lower my eyes to my desk,

carved into the wood, the letters sharp and crooked as scorpion legs:
ALICIA RIVERS IS A DYKE HOE

and it takes me a full minute to realize
really realize
that it's my name on this desk
and despite the pit in my stomach
widening into a chasm
part of me wants to laugh
because someone in this school
thinks saying this about me
is going to break my heart

As if this is the worst thing that they can do
the worst thing that has been done
the worst thing that can be said about me.

Listen kid, if you think this is bad
you should hear what I say
about myself.

I take a picture and send it to Deja

Alicia: I think my ISAP desk is calling me a slut
Deja: lolol
Deja: wait is this real
Alicia: 🪦
Deja: the fuck? whose ass do I have to beat
Alicia: you told me you've never been in a fight
Deja: first time for everything
Alicia: don't waste your fists on a hoe
Deja: who else would I use them for?
Deja: also, what is a dyke hoe? specifically?
Alicia: lololol

Deja invites me to her family game night

and I say no
because I think

she's just
being nice

and the
only thing

worse than
senseless cruelty

is fake
kindness

and I don't
want her

to think
she owes

me anything
but

the
truth.

Things They Call Me: A List

- Slut
- Hoe, a derivative of Whore
- Whore, obviously
- Girl with daddy issues
- Attention whore, which is different than just Whore, apparently
- Only Good for One Thing
- Lightbulb ("how many does it take to screw"—it doesn't even make sense)
- Lunchbox ("you can fit everything in it"—this one is at least somewhat creative)
- Pathetic
- Whoremione (I laughed at this one)
- Liar
- Dyke (does that apply if you're bi?)
- Dyke hoe

Pre-slut

I remember when other people were the slut
before me.

I remember sitting in the cafeteria
when Sarah still went here

when everyone was talking about Taryn Billups
and how she supposedly gave two guys
a blow job on the same day.

Maybe at the same time.

Now it's my turn. It's hard to say
where it began—if I slept with one guy
too many, or if the Colonel's touch
left a stench like gasoline
that the whole school
can smell.

Rumors are like wildfire:
a little breath
and the flames are running
catching
burning

The only difference is
wildfire burns
everything in its path,
and a rumor about a slut
only burns one.

We're going on a field trip to the history museum

and I end up on the same bus as Deja.
I try my hardest to sit at the front but she sees me
before I can duck down—yells my name
relentlessly
until I make my way to the back with her
and her friends.

She lets me have the window
and allows me to be ignored
but in closer proximity.

Her friends are loud and sing songs
I don't know, and some that I do.

She overhears me murmuring to Chaka Khan
a name I only know because of ISAP,
and she bumps me with her elbow,
beaming. We sit close, singing low,
and then she bumps me again, pointing:

In the seat across the aisle and one up,
Melody Ross is sitting with Matt Wheaton,
her boyfriend of two days—
they have a sweatshirt over
their legs. Her hand is under it,
in Matt's lap, moving.

Not slick, Deja whispers, laughing,
and it doesn't occur to me that this
can be funny, that some things
can be done by some people

and not by others
and the rules change all the time.

When I crack up, Deja thinks I'm laughing
at Melody and Matt, but really
I'm laughing at the lightbulb in my head
and how it only took one person to screw it in.

I keep seeing Geneva in the museum

and it feels more like science
and less like history
the way I end up in the same exhibits
as Geneva,
the way we end up side by side
studying ancient suits of armor,
as if a magnet has been installed
between my ribs and draws me
toward something in her made
of iron or nickel.

I thought they were all made of metal,
she says, and I think she's reading my mind
until I realize she's talking about the armor,
the way the exhibit says some civilizations
made armor out of plants, of animal, of wood.

Some are made of bone too, I say, pointing.

And then she's looking at me, her hand raised,
and she takes a single finger and presses it against
the back of my hand, saying
And some are made of skin.

Girls are either straight, gay, or whores.

Even people who are supposed to know better
think this.

The world is so eager to put people into boxes
they can understand.

The ideal box: straight, of course.
Less ideal, but understandable at this point: gay

But bi?

If you're a girl who's bi, you're a slut who
can't make up her mind and just wants
an excuse to fuck
everyone.
See also: attention whore
See also: whore, whore

If you're a boy who's bi, you're really gay
but don't have the guts to admit it,
because what REAL MAN has slept with women
but still wants other men?

Then, if you're a girl, there's the best box:
not having sex with anyone at all.
(Too late.)

Algebra of "Why boys?"

Number of dreams I've had about kissing girls > number of boys
    I've kissed

I hear Sarah in my head always
like one of her church's angels
shaking her finger and her head:

You don't even like him.
If you don't like it why
do it?

Define your terms, Sarah.
Him and *it* don't balance
the equation
        or whatever.

Apples and oranges.

I don't think this is about math
to begin with.

It's about hunger
and if boys are apples
and girls are oranges,
the apples hang lower on the tree,
are easier to reach.

Is that the only reason?
Is there something wrong with me?

I fall asleep on the bus back to school,

too many half nights in my bed at home
catching up with me
and powerless against the rocking
of the bus, the quiet melody of low conversation,
everyone too tired after walking around the museum
to sing.

I wake up as we pull back into school,
my head jolting up from Deja's shoulder.
She laughs and says *You're just like my sister.*
Always asleep in the car

and I'm embarrassed, not just for the little bit
of drool at the corner of my mouth
but at the rush of happy and sad
that I feel at being someone's sister
once more.

My mother is waiting for me in the kitchen.

The door isn't even closed yet and she's shouting:

A man was here asking for you. He said you're his
girlfriend. What the hell is going on, Alicia?
Who was that? He was as old as your cousins!
He had to have been twenty-five!
What are you hiding from me?

And I have too many questions of my own
that I can't ask:
What did he look like?
What was he driving?
Because if I were "normal"
there would only be one answer
to the question of "who"
but instead I can think of a few,
although I don't know why the hell
any of them would knock
on my door in broad daylight.

It must have been one of David's friends
fucking around, I snap, *I don't have*
a boyfriend

and it feels good to at least tell this small
truth. I watch her face relax,

do math,
the likelihood of my brother
having friends who would do something
like this outweighing the probability
of her quiet, hardworking daughter
stepping out of line and into a shadowy lie.

When her back is turned again, accepting
all my nothing,
I feel a knot in my throat
not because I want to cry
but because I want to scream

to tell her
that a wolf was at her door
and she's yelling at me
instead.

Text from a random at 9pm

Him: I came by your house today, I didn't know you lived with your
    parents
Alicia: I'm 16 of course I do
Him: I didn't know you were 16
Alicia: You didn't ask
Him: Wow
Him: Are you busy tonight?

You'd think I would stay home

after my mother freaked out,
after my secret life almost came
unraveled.

But frozen in my head
is the picture of rage
painted on my mother's face
when it dawned on her
that maybe her daughter
was wading in dark water.

It makes me want to stay on land.
But now I hear her in the garage
not crying, but cursing at my father,
and my brother's door is dark,
and a sinkhole opens in my chest.

The random's name is Johnathan and he picks me up
in a light blue Hyundai. He's in college,
not quite twenty-five like my mother thought.

But he has his own apartment
and he takes me there
where I wade into that dark water,
sometimes looking at my phone
to see when it will start glowing and screaming,
my father coming to the house to check on us
and finding me gone.

But it never does.
He never does.

In ISAP for skipping art: Part (?)

We are allowed up for a bathroom break
all at once
so Mr. West can escort us
with the help of Mr. Upton, the security guard.

Except this time, Mr. West waves
everyone out—when I get to the door
he holds his arm out to block me

and my heart turns into a rat
fast and dirty
looking for a hole to hide in
or maybe a limb to chew off.

I stare at the door starting
to swing closed, wondering
if this will be the day I howl.

But then his arm reaches out again, catches
the door, props it open. Turns back inside
the classroom, gestures for me
to follow.

He comes to the desk I was sitting in
last week, the one I sent Deja a photo of.
The words are still there, of course, and we both
stare at them. I feel the heat on my face
like it's hell.

This you? he says, nodding down, his frown
so deep I can't see the bottom.

I nod too.

He frowns more, staring me in my eyes,
and then his hand lifts, offering me something silver.

A razor blade.

Here, he says. *Scratch that shit out.*

I reach, and my fingers are shaking,
and I take the blade and use it
to render the words invisible, slow
at first and then faster, turning
it all into a scar.

He watches, shaking his head.
Fuck these kids, he says,
then goes back to his desk
and nods to Diana Ross.

If only a razor blade fixed everything.

This is not an allusion to suicide
or even mass violence.

I'm just wishing
I could take that silver metal
in my fist

and scratch it through my life
until every ugly thing that has been true

is no longer.

Blake Felipe was staring at me today in the cafeteria

with no smile on her mouth, even as her friends
whirled and chirped around her the way
happy girls do. I was sitting by the windows
imagining I was one of the red leaves blowing toward oblivion
    outside
and she was at the table that she was born to sit at

but for some reason she was staring
at me, even when I switched to the other side of the table,
even when I looked down
and then up again,
even when I turned my back
and then glanced in her direction.

It's not like high school movies,
where the cool girls are rattlesnakes
and girls like me are tripped
into plates full of ketchup. Rather
there is a wall that separates us
a line we don't cross,
a beach of untouched sand stretching between us,

and Blake staring at me
the way she was
stepped upon that beach
though I don't know why.

I haven't slept with her boyfriend,
but maybe one of her friends
has a boyfriend I slept with
without realizing it.

By the time I look again, she's gone
but I can't get the expression on her face
out of my head
even if I don't know what it meant.

Mariah the misanthrope is crying in drive-thru

and I tell her to sit on the floor of the booth
before customers see her and wonder
what the fuck is going on.

Terry the pervy manager has gone to the bank
to get us change for the hundreds in our drawers
so Mariah sits at my feet while I take orders
for beef and cheddars while also
running the cash register. I glance down
at her occasionally and can't see her face
buried in her hands. Every few minutes
I pass her down stiff brown napkins,
the Meat Palace logo catching her tears,

and I almost say
I didn't think you were the kind of girl who cried
but being a misanthrope
doesn't mean anything
when it comes to
a broken heart.

My brother asks me to bring home mozzarella sticks

and I smile, even if I'm annoyed
that he waited until 7:58
when I clock out
at 8:00. But I drop the sticks
into the boiling grease,
stare down at them as they
transform.

I think I'm probably losing my mind
at this point, comparing
myself to mozzarella sticks,

but how can I not
when they are submerged
in burn, transforming,
when Sarah said
I'm going to hell?

I didn't expect Justin to be at our house, but I should have.

He has become like a mole on my brother's face:
I'm having trouble remembering what David
looks like without Justin
slumped by his side, always the same smell
coming off him in waves:

Weed and cats
Weed and cats
Weed and cats

I don't think my brother's gay—
he called me a carpet muncher
when I told him I had a crush
on a girl in ninth grade—but I guess
David being gay doesn't mean
David can't also be cruel.

But I can't explain why else Justin
would have turned my brother into Velcro.
They're standing there in the kitchen
when I walk in, and the smell of cigarettes

tells me my mother is in the garage, smoking
and probably/definitely crying.

I stare at my brother and he stares back,
nods at the bag.
"Is that for us?"

"No," I say.
"It's for you."

"Same thing" says Justin
and he doesn't say it the way a boyfriend would
not flirty or funny.
He says it the way kudzu would speak
of the car it has swallowed:
We're the same thing. This is mine now.

MONDAY, DECEMBER 3
In the morning I usually avoid the mirror:

I don't think I actually look like myself until noon
after the puffiness of a half-slept night has worn off.

But today I look in the full-length mirror that hangs on my wall
standing there in my bra and underwear that don't match,
my hair piled on top of my head. My legs had gotten skinny
for a while, with no track, no weight room.
They look like they've changed again now:
the result of my daily sprints to the bus stop, perhaps,
or maybe all the Meat Palace.

Staring at my legs
I remember how they once felt
carrying me around the track,

one stride at a time, one breath
at a time. The never-ending
strike   swish   strike
as my legs carried me on and on,

part of a beautiful, complicated machine.

My body felt
powerful
capable
brimming with joy,
part of me.

Now I feel like Dorothy,
tumbled out of a tornado
into a strange land.

I don't recognize any part
of myself. When I stare too long
at any one extremity
hands
ankles
I feel a swell of something
like grief, words in my head
repeating

Those aren't mine
Those aren't mine
I'm not mine

When I leave for school, Justin and my brother are sleeping on couches

the TV still on. My mother's car is gone
so she must have gone to work.

That means she walked right past them
and didn't wake them,
didn't reach for the remote
to shut everything up.

I imagine her pausing at the door,
looking back at what her life has become
and saying
Fuck it.

On the bus, I stare down at my khaki legs

wrinkled and with a grease stain near the knee.
I wear the same pants to school as I do to work.
I'm sure my classmates sit in physics and wonder
where the smell of beef is wafting from
but I don't care. I heard someone say once

that girls don't dress for boys, that they dress
for other girls, that we're more interested in impressing
our own sex than the opposite. Sometimes I hear
a game show host in my head say things
like an announcement over the speaker at Walmart:
Heteronormative, ladies and gentlemen,
the voice says now,
what about everybody gay?
Everyone neither lady
nor gentleman?

Either way
I don't dress for anyone.
More so, I dress for no one.

Boys don't actually care
what you wear, just what's under
it, and they really don't care
about that either if they're being honest,
and they rarely are.

The new girl/Geneva is sitting with someone in the cafeteria

A boy.
He's white with a nice haircut—a senior
I think, with a name like
Nathaniel
or Sebastian
or Alexander.

Something long
like his eyelashes

and I feel a stab of something
green in my stomach,
another kind of envy
than the plant that blooms
when I stare at Blake Felipe.

This plant has ragged edges
and I tell myself it's because
Geneva and the boy each have someone
to sit with in the cafeteria
and not because

they're sitting
so close.

Guess what, Sarah?

I'm sinning again.
This time Jacob Wheeler
wants to give me a ride
to work.

We used to run track
together—he was more into
cross-country, if I remember
right.

He catches me at the bus stop
and says *hey.*

We're not even out
of the parking lot
before his hand
appears on
my thigh.

Jacob Wheeler doesn't actually try to get in my pants.

When his hand went to my leg
he was trying to wipe off
the grease stain near my knee.

I thought it was from my car
he says, and sounds embarrassed.

It's grease, I say.
From work.

Oh. Okay.

We ride in silence. He seems
to already know where to go—
I guess my Meat Palace shirt
is direction enough.

We're pulling into the parking lot
when he finally speaks
asks me why

I don't run track anymore:

I was so good
I was so fast
Didn't I set a record

Yes I was
Yes I was
Yes I did

But I don't say it out loud: those words
have sharp edges and snag
in my throat. Instead I say

I just have other priorities right now
and am out of the car
before he can ask what they are,
before he can see
the tears that emerge
for the first time since
the Day.
Thanks for the ride, though

Work is a good distraction

especially when Stephanie is the shift manager.

She says *Terry will be in later,*

almost as a warning,

and I say *But not yet?*

> And she shakes her head.
>
> Mariah comes out of drive-thru
>
> mascara intact
>
> and says
>
> *Crank it.*

Stephanie turns up the lobby music

even though there are two old ladies

in a booth and they look

offended by the three girls

> dancing by the soda machine,
>
> one of them—me—
>
> singing into a mop.

Snapshot of a(n) (im)perfect girl

If someone were to peek through the Meat Palace window
at me doing fast-food karaoke
and this was all they knew of my life

and this was the only part of me they ever saw,
they would think that everything was fine:

That this snapshot,
this moment,

was a perfect teenage girl
living a perfect teenage life

and while I am here
with this song playing
that is what I will pretend
to be.

I'm not scheduled for Saturday and Sunday

and I ask Stephanie why.

You requested off a long time ago, I thought?
Don't you have a wedding to go to?

Stephanie knows my life better than I do.

Tomorrow morning we're going to Cincinnati
for my dad's sister's third wedding.

My mom isn't coming
and my brother is.

I try to imagine what this car ride will be like,
stare at the floor I just mopped

and entertain the idea
of slipping, breaking my leg.

No point.

I would still have to go, even though a cast
would ruin Aunt Linda's photos.

My father is always on time.

He's waiting at the end of the driveway,
not bothering to come and knock.

My mother seems relieved to watch us go,
especially my brother.
I imagine her fumigating the house
while we're gone,
trying to get the smell
of weed and cats
out of the couch Justin lounges on
like it's his own.

David gets in the front seat and I don't even argue.
I imagine the backseat as a ditch
on a battlefield, safe-ish
from flying artillery.

But no one argues. My dad is an expert
at pretending everything is fine,
and my brother actually smiles,
tells Dad a story from school.

I should be happy, relieved
that the two hours to Cincinnati
are peaceful, but I can't help but feel
everyone in the car is wearing a mask,
especially me.

The dress Aunt Linda wants me to wear is pink

and looks terrible with the neon poison of my head.

Is there . . . anything you can do about your hair?
She says it with her mouth twisting in that same way
my father's does.

Nope, it's permanent, and I turn away before
she can see me smile.

My mother hates the color of my hair
but I think she'd be happy that it pisses off Aunt Linda.

They never liked each other.

The thing about weddings

is that everyone gets drunk, and no one notices
if the teenagers do too.

I sneak a little to drink but I've never liked alcohol
and leave it sitting on someone's table.

I find my brother at the edge of the hotel ballroom
watching my dad's family make fools of themselves

on the dance floor while Aunt Linda walks around
posing for pictures. Her dress follows her
like an ivory puddle, and after I stand there
next to David for a full ten minutes
he says out of nowhere

Remember when Aunt Linda hosted the family reunion?

Yes.

She looks like she made that dress out of the curtains in her bathroom.

and we both laugh forever
remembering that bathroom
    all yellow-white lace
    all chipped porcelain statues of Jesus and lambs
    all damp hand towels with tattered edges

we laugh louder than the music
and it feels so good to be
on the same team
even for a moment
even at the expense
of someone else.

While everyone is slow dancing

I stand out on the balcony alone, without a coat,
even though it's December and the chill has set in.

I look out at Cincinnati and think about moving here—
moving anywhere.

College is on everyone's mind, and next year
I'll have to start applying.

Or at least pretend to. Currently I plan to lie
and say I didn't get in anywhere.

Maybe I'll work at Meat Palace my entire life.
    There's a woman named Debbie at work who has.

Cincinnati has Meat Palace.

In the back of my head there's a whisper

but it's not exactly words.

The feeling of my feet striking track
The sound of my breath in my own ears
The slow crawl of sweat at the nape of my neck
The swing of my ponytail at the top of my shoulders

The way the whole world fades around me,
my lungs the only adversary, and also my only partner,
my muscles part of that beautiful, complicated machine that

Lets
Me
Run

And then the whisper becomes words:
You could run again.
You could run in college.
Coach Young always said you could.
You could go to the Olympics.

And that's where I smash the whisper with my fist,
because sometimes it seems absurd to wish
for things I know I don't deserve.

How could I?
Look what I am.

On the way home, my dad is glowing

the way he always does when he has been around his family.

I should really move to Cincinnati, he says.
I should. My whole family is there.

Not us, David says, and I'm so shocked I twist
the hem of my shirt in my hands, saying nothing.

You can come visit me, Dad says, so cheerful.
He has already decided.

He has already decided to extricate himself
from the wound of this former life.

Linda was so beautiful, wasn't she? he says.
What a wedding.

What a third *wedding,* David says,
and my hands go on twisting.

What's the big deal? Dad laughs.
She's a woman who knows what she wants.
Sometimes you have to kiss a few frogs
before you find a prince.

I wonder what he would think of my frogs.
I wonder if he would still call me princess.

Cincinnati sucks, David says,
All they have is chili.

Only then do I speak:
With noodles, I say.

With noodles, David says.

Sunday nights

Are like

Waiting for a bus to hit you

125

                              Standing in a baseball field
                    watching a ball hurtling toward your forehead

Walking through a desert about to drink
your last drop of water

                                        Climbing a fence knowing
                                   there's a tiger on the other side.

                    Not a tiger.
                    A wolf.
                    Always a wolf.

Monday it finally happens:

Someone's boyfriend told their girlfriend
that he had messed around with me
while they were "on a break."

A girl named Audrey who I've spoken to
only once comes up to my locker
with a lot of foul names
but no fists, and I've encountered
enough of the former already
to be able to turn my back.

My shoulders absorb the rest of her words:

That's why he's my boyfriend
but you're just a skank.
He doesn't care about you.

That's the only time I say anything back:
Audrey, what makes you think I care about him?

It's not until she walks away that I see the note

Slipped into the grille of my locker, white and creased
like a fancy dinner napkin.

When I open it, the words are blue, sweeping
and smeared:

I know about him

I almost laugh
because apparently Audrey
isn't the only one whose HIM
I have crossed paths with

and somewhere underneath my layers
of shell, of skin-turned-armor,
something raw and pulpy
like the inside of a clam
twinges

I should feel bad
I should feel something

Mostly what I feel is relieved
that all these random HIMs
distract me from the HIM
that's as specific as
a scalpel.

But there's something else—

the blue ink, the circles for i's.

It's the only kind of note I've gotten
this year, and an eel
twitches in the bog of my gut.

Something that wants me to notice.
Something I'm not ready to look at.
Something I can't bear to see.

Things They Call Me: An Updated List

- Slut
- Hoe, a derivative of Whore
- Whore, obviously
- Girl with daddy issues
- Attention whore, which is different than just Whore, apparently
- Only Good for One Thing
- Lightbulb
- Lunchbox
- Pathetic
- Whoremione
- Liar
- Dyke
- *Skank*

I don't have ISAP for two days and it feels like returning to Earth from a space shuttle.

Mrs. Fisher says,
I'd almost forgotten what you looked like!

And I don't know if she means it to be funny
or cruel

but the class laughs
either way.

Texts with Deja

Deja: Mrs. Fisher just mad that her ass looks like a pancake in those pocketless parachutes she struts around in

Alicia: I think she likes the pancake look

Deja: speaking of pancakes, come with me on Saturday to this new brunch spot

Alicia: . . . brunch

Deja: Breakfast + lunch dummy

Alicia: I know what brunch is! But that sounds so . . .

Deja: Bougie?

Alicia: lol yes

Deja: So wear a dress. Come on it will be fun

Alicia: Saturday?

Deja: Don't tell me you have to work. Meat Palace doesn't serve breakfast

Alicia: Yes we do!

Deja: Omg don't say WE

Alicia: lmao fine

Deja: good

I run to the bus stop after school

but I'm early and my shift doesn't start until
four. I pause, wondering
if I could make it there in forty-five minutes
if I walked fast.
Or if I jogged.

If I ran.

I hook my thumbs in my backpack loops
and start down Baker.

With the backpack on my back,
even empty of books,
it feels like conditioning:

My mind races back to freshman year
when Coach Young had us run
and run
and run

Relays, sprints, v-sits, butt-kicks, box jumps

My muscles seem to twitch inside my khakis
remembering, knowing, missing.

The memories feel like an injection,
fill me to buzzing.

It buzzes all the way up to my head,
the afternoons spent in the sun
and then when the leaves began to sweep down,
running the halls on rainy days.

It was raining the first time, That Day last March.
That's how I knew the Colonel was still in his classroom,
how I saw the always-open door.

That memory pushes all the buzzing down,
out. My muscles begin to ache, feel heavy.

I stop running.
I get to work late.

I smell cat and weed as soon as I get home

and know immediately that Justin is here,
that my brother has returned home from Cincinnati
and picked up right where he left off.

Is Mom at work? I ask.
Her car isn't here, so she's somewhere.

He shrugs, doesn't look at me.
He and Justin are on laptops
playing a game involving orcs
and elves. I can hear the screams
of damsels in distress.

Justin glances up, eyeing me
as if wondering why I'm still here.
Here where I live
Here in my house
Here in my own home

He sees me staring back says
Can I help you?

Don't you have somewhere to be?
and I try to make my voice as sharp
as I feel, imagine myself a thorn
in his shoe. He just goes on staring,
silent, and I hate the look
in his eyes, the way he makes me feel
small, exposed. I hate the way
my brother sees nothing.

Eventually I look away and I go to my room,
close the door so the smell of Justin
can't sneak into my carpet.

I lock the door for good measure.

Texts with my mother

Her: I'm at dinner with some friends
Alicia: Who?
Her: Old friends from my last school
Alicia: Oh okay. I'm home just fyi
Her: Of course you are—it's 10 o'clock! ;)
Alicia: haha yeah

It never occurs to her that I may be somewhere other than where I say I am.

She doesn't even know
that Sarah and I are no longer
friends. I wonder sometimes
when I use Sarah as an alibi
if one day my mom will run into her
at the grocery store
and every lie, every alibi,
will explode right there
in the produce section
like an overripe melon.

My mother works as the secretary
at an elementary school two miles
away. She switched from a middle school
because everyone
from the kids to the principal
was "raised in a barn,"
according to her.

She never talked about friends,
she never talked about anyone
except her boss who was a functioning

alcoholic and would sip from a flask
between parent conferences.

"Dinner with friends."
It has never occurred to me
that my mother may be somewhere
other than where she says
she is.

She's probably dating and I would be happy

at the idea of her kicking my father
to the curb of her mind

except the idea that she is at dinner
holding hands while I am floating

in the silent, empty world
my life has become

makes my whole room blur
with something like tears

but that might also be nausea.
My mother feels alone, just her

and the garage, the lawn chair,
the phone pressed against her face

while my grandma tells her she "never
should have married that silver-spoon shithead."

Loneliness has a way of turning forests
into trees: the whole disappears,

a single trunk remaining. I think again
of kudzu, the way the vines swarm

up the trunk and swallow everything
whole. Something is eating me alive

and right now I want to call my mom
but my mouth is full of vines

and in the end I just lie down
to sleep.

THURSDAY, DECEMBER 6
Mr. Hudson asks where my homework is

and he must be surprised when I laugh, because his eyebrows
shoot up to the middle of his forehead.

I slept for only three hours last night—
the rest of the time I spent shifting,
sure I felt fingers at the edge of my shirt,
prying at the top of the sheet.

My best dreams are about running
so fast the wind can't catch me.
My worst dreams are about trying to run
and my muscles collapsing in columns of wet cement,
wolves snapping at my heels.

So when Mr. Hudson asks where my homework is
all I can do is laugh because wearing a mask
feels impossible when everything is this wrong.

He asks why I'm laughing and I'm so tired
I'm honest:

For a history teacher,
you're pretty terrible at learning from it.
I haven't turned in homework in four weeks—

what the hell makes you think
you're going to get it today?

He'd been teaching about this or that war
and now bombs drop all over his face.

I'm in ISAP five minutes later,
Mr. West shaking his head, pointing at a seat.
I don't bother playing spades on my phone.
Aretha Franklin sings me to sleep.

Mr. West escorts us to the cafeteria for lunch

Where we have to sit at the ISAP table,
not allowed to talk
to the general population
only eat in silence among each other
which is perfect for me.

But over the course of those thirty minutes
I find three separate pairs of eyes
watching me:

1. Blake Felipe. Again. Her expression is cold. She's with another
   senior, collecting box lunches for a senior trip. She stares at me
   the entire way to the door, eyes like smooth ice.
2. Audrey. She sits next to her again-boyfriend, smirking at me like
   a cat with cream. She doesn't understand that if she is a cat, I am
   a lizard, and lizards don't give a fuck about cream.
3. Geneva. She doesn't stare like the other two. Her eyes wander
   like two searchlights crossing a swamp, but they always
   come back
   to me.

Geneva stops to say hi.

She has already dropped her tray off
and stands with her hands empty,
one reaching as if to tap my shoulder
but I'm already turning around
when she arrives at my table.

Keep moving, young lady, Mr. West says,
These students are in ISAP.

He says it just as her lips are parting to speak
and they twist closed again like a shy blossom
when she hears his voice.

In the end she just waves with one
of those delicate painter's hands.

I wave back but I want to kiss
her palm.

If Sundays are:

a bus
a baseball
a desert,

        Fridays are:
        a horse and carriage
        a Nerf ball
        an oasis

Not without risk
but a hell of a lot safer
than the other stuff.

Tomorrow I'm getting brunch with Deja

and I feel more nervous than I do when I'm opening the door
to a car I've never been in.

In the car scenario
everything there is to fear
I have already seen.

In the brunch scenario
I open myself up to a different kind of trauma:

the Sarah kind,
the kind that slices past the skin
and all the way to the heart.

There should be a special word
for the kind of heartbreak
that comes not from a lover
but from a friend.

Brunch is like breakfast but everyone is more awake.

Everything in the restaurant is made up of bright colors,
including the people, everyone more dressed up
than they would be for breakfast.

It's called Chicken or the Egg
and there's a paleo section on the menu
that I'm staring at—trying to understand
what paleo actually is—when Deja
and her friends arrive.

I knew it wouldn't be just the two
of us but I still feel awkward,

like Pinocchio string-walking
to the booth we're led to,
sitting down among
real girls, flesh and blood
beside dull wood.

But Deja is a butterfly
and to her we are all flowers:
her attentions flutter between us,
bringing us together.

I'm glad I wore something
other than my work pants
for once.

Brunch conversations

Deja: *One more year and we can shake this place off like dandruff!*

Amanda: *Eww! I'm eating! Why are you so nasty?*

Deja: *The school is nasty, not me! Right, Alicia?*

Alicia: *You can get shampoo for dandruff. I don't think there's a cure for Marshall.*

Denise: *That's high school in general though.*

Deja: *Nah, there's something extra trifling about Marshall. Can't put my finger on it.*

Amanda: *Maybe if you weren't in ISAP all the time . . . !*

Deja: *When I'm in ISAP it's to make a statement. Alicia knows. They're always policing Black girls' hair but never say nothing to Alicia about hers.*

Amanda: *Maybe because Alicia doesn't give teachers no lip!*

Isis: *(arriving late) You must not know Alicia very well!*

We all laugh.

Even me, after what Isis said.
It's funny because Isis doesn't know me either
but she knows something *about* me,

something that has nothing to do
with whose car I've been in
whose floor my bra has been on

but rather
the fire that comes out
of my mouth when Mrs. Fisher
or Mr. Hudson looks at me
the wrong way.

We all order variations of pancakes
and it's nice to have this new aspect
of my reputation
precede me.

Deja's friends are nothing like Sarah.

They say what they think and silences
are only because someone is checking their phone.
It's nice to be around people who tell you what they're thinking
without having to guess,
without having to stare at the gaps
and wonder what's behind them,
inside them.

Everyone says Andrea is dating Mike now,
Denise says, pouring a cascade of amber over her pancakes.

He doesn't act like he has a girlfriend, I say,
and all eyes hover on my face, eyebrows raised.

What does that *mean?* A smile starts
at the corner of Denise's lip like spilled syrup.

Nothing, I say. If she's spilled syrup I feel
like I've spilled ketchup
or cranberry.
Blood.

Something that stains.

But Deja laughs, a sound like cracking ice,
and it melts a piece of something in me:

I'm not proud of everything I do
but her laugh tells me maybe
there's a different thing to feel
than shame.

Deja's friends aren't mine yet.

It sounds bad but I've never really
hung out with Black girls before,
not because I didn't want to
but because it just didn't happen—

I learned about gerrymandering
on TikTok and I know it's about elections
but sometimes it feels like our lives
are gerrymandered too—my middle school
as white as cave fish, and Marshall
not much different. They split

the "gifted" kids off in their own classes
but Deja is the smartest person
I've ever met and she's not in them.

Until now it's just been Sarah—
Sarah by my side since
second grade. I'm the kind of person
who has always been satisfied
with one good friend, even when the "good"
starts to wear thin. That's the problem
with having all your eggs in one basket
as my grandma would've said. One breaks
and then what do you have?

She never actually said what you would have,
but the answer is a lonely mess.

And it's too soon to call Deja's friends
mine
but as we leave brunch, all of us walking
for the same bus stop,
I allow myself to watch them, imagining
what could be.

They talk about church but the Bible doesn't fall out of their
    mouths like fists.
They talk about boyfriends and boundaries and basketball.
They call each other on their shit, they laugh and laugh.

Their hairstyles are the balance of math
and poetry: there are specific rules being followed,
a formula I don't quite know, but there is the rhythm and loveliness
of poems—color and light and texture

all coming together in the form of braids
and swoops and waves.

Deja sees me watching and smiles:
What? Do I have something on my face?

Just your face, I say, which is something
I used to say to my brother, and him to me,
but now I'm saying it to her and she's laughing
and I wonder
if this is how family
is chosen.

The westbound bus comes first.

Everyone catches it but me and Isis.
We wave when it pulls off and I expect awkwardness
to flutter down from the sky and land between us
like a flock of birds. But Isis is on the dance team,
peppy, all teeth and eyes.
She looks me up and down while we shiver, says
Can you dance? We need two more people.

When I tell her I don't know, she laughs: *How do you not know if
    you can dance?*

I've never tried.

*Well honestly that probably means you can't right now,
but it doesn't mean you can't ever.*

We laugh at that, at the erasure of a fairy tale: the lie
that one can Cinderella (verb) a skill:
rags of rhythm to the riches
of the complicated routines I've seen her team execute.

She eyes me again.
Do you do sports, though? You've got body!
What do you do with it?

I hate that my first thought is Adam
the Colonel
randoms
in my head like pollution,
clouding my thoughts.

Deja says you used to run track, she says.
She doesn't notice the left my brain has taken
in the traffic of this conversation. *What happened?*

A lot, I answer.

An injury? Whatever happened, you've gotta rehab that.
Some things just take time but
you'll be running again soon.

The wounds she imagines are so different than what are.

I don't know how she can be right.
The break inside me
is not a sprained ankle.

My mom isn't at home the next two nights

but David is, with Justin and the other carpet stains
he calls friends. I wait for him to come upstairs
for more snacks to ask him:

Is Mom working extra shifts?

She said she was meeting friends, he says,
not looking at me.

What friends?

How should I know?

I feel like the mother of a teenager,
sit in her chair waiting for her to come home,
ignore the texts from guys on my phone
while I stare at the door.

9pm. 10pm. I have to sleep
or waking up to catch the bus
will be impossible. I send her a text

I waited up for you

then turn off my phone.

The new girl/Geneva is waiting at my locker Monday morning.

I see her at the end of the hall like a comet
smoldering into Earth's atmosphere.

I almost turn around, break
for the exit.

But she sees me before
I can disappear.

I'm drawn to her like a worm
to warm soil.

Hi, she says. *I was wondering
if I could ask you something.*

I brace myself. What question
could possibly exist

that would bring her into
my universe?

Sure, I say.
Sure.

Could you maybe not *cuss out Mrs. Fisher
today? Because I'd like to sit with you*

*at lunch, and you being in ISAP
makes that really hard.*

I don't know how long I stare
at her, waiting for words to come.

Her smile answers anyway.

Good, she says.

I bite my tongue when Mrs. Fisher says

Look who's here!
as if the reason I'm in ISAP every day isn't her,
as if every day she doesn't dangle herself
like a red cape before a bull. Today her eyes
sweep down over me, looking for uniform
infractions, settle for a moment on the stain
near my knee. I go to my desk.

My classmates ignore me, except Shane
Balter, who flips paper wads at my hunched
shoulders. It is incredible to me
that boys are allowed to be boys
for so long, while girls
are made women years before
we're ready.

Thoughts on "maturity"

Teachers, parents, family, strangers
always call girls
"mature."

Serious
stern
responsible
girls.

Thoughtful
reliable
trustworthy
girls.

As I got older, my body pushing
against the inside of my cartoon T-shirts,
mature took on a different definition.

You're so mature for your age
said the man at the gas station
when I came inside to pay for my dad.

*You look so much older. You act
so much older* whispers every man
trying to convince me that giving them
my phone number is appropriate,
explaining how we are the same.

From first grade to eleventh
when a boy has hit me, screamed
in my direction, goofed off while the girls
sat in their seats and obeyed,
I have been told
Girls mature faster than boys

and when I was younger I would take it
as a compliment but now that I'm sixteen
and I've seen the way it all plays out
year after year, I've realized

it's not a compliment—
it's a scam.

Scam or not

I keep my mouth shut in Mrs. Fisher's class, even
when she tells me she's taking points off
my homework for using a pen
instead of pencil.

I stare at her back.
At least I did it
At least I tried
At least I'm here

and I can feel the curse words
bubbling in my throat like oil

but on the other side of this hour
is the cafeteria
and in it waits
Geneva.

She already has her food when I get there

and I'm too anxious to eat, but I slide through
the line anyway, just to give myself time
to collect myself, to gather
all these feelings like fish into a net.

The white guy she sits with sometimes
Nathaniel/Sebastian/Alexander
is nowhere in sight

and I wonder if she's dumped him
or if he's sick
or maybe he's in ISAP
and she's traded us out
like Pokémon cards.

The seat across from her is cool
against my butt and I focus on that,
not the heat of her eyes
like two lamps over a lizard tank.

She smiles vaguely, like she's surprised
I'm here, or maybe pleased, or maybe
like she forgot she'd even asked me
to come. *Hey* she says, and I say *hey*
back, and she says, *So,*
here you are. Alicia.

I nod, swallow back the swelling
in my throat at the sound of my name
from those lips.

I haven't kissed a girl since Renée.
Am I still bi if I've kissed a dozen
(or more) guys
and only one girl? Am I still bi
if one kiss has filled my dreams
for four years, but not my life?

I'm Geneva, she says, and I say *I know,*
and she takes a bite of her apple

with a curve of her lips like I have told
a very clever joke.

Well now we know each other, she says,
and smiles more when I say *Yeah.*

One of Geneva's eyes is squintier than the other

and her nose has the slightest angle.

She doesn't pluck the hair between
her eyebrows, and one is perpetually raised.

She clenches her teeth on one side,
so her jaw looks sharper on the right.

Her chin is the only thing that's mirror-
image: sharp and short.

Someone in art history said that symmetry
is beauty
and that person—
    whoever he was—
was an idiot.

But I still cut art.

The promise of Geneva and her paint-covered hands
is sometimes enough to pass the Colonel's classroom
but when I aim my feet for studio,
they take me to the library instead
and so I follow, wandering through the aisles,
feeling like a raccoon avoiding porch light
as I evade teachers walking laps
to keep an eye on their students.

That's when I find Deja, tucked
into the back of the history stacks,
knees drawn up to her chest, eyes
flowing over the pages.
She doesn't even notice me
until I sit down, when she jumps,
then smiles. *Let me guess,*
she says. *Cutting.*

I shrug and we read, her *The Color Purple*
and me a random book I pull from the shelf
about Greek mythology, flipping
past tridents and Pegasus, everyone shirtless
and carrying either lambs or lightning.

When I get to Medusa I pause
because I know her name but not much else,
only that the snakes that are growing
from her head are less frightening
than the hell in her eyes
and the book is mostly text
but it feels like looking
into a mirror.

"What's that about?"

Deja is peering over my shoulder at Medusa's
snakes and I whisper the short caption:

**One of the three monstrous Gorgons, generally
described as winged human females
living in caves, venomous snakes in place of hair.**

**Those who gazed into her eyes
would be turned to stone.**

Deja nods, familiar, and we both
agree that, if we could, there are a number
of people at Marshall who we would gladly
stare into statues. I ask about her book,
which she holds up, looking thoughtful:
>   *I think you'd like it,* she says.

Why?

>   *Because I think these ladies
>   love each other.*

Oh. I mean . . . okay. Why do you *like it?*

>   *Because it's about a Black woman
>   finding her freedom. It kinda reads
>   like poetry.*

Do you write poetry?

>   *A little. I write about love
>   but it's hard sometimes. I think
>   my ideas about love are different
>   than everybody else's.*

How?

>   *People seem to think so much
>   about skin. I don't want anyone
>   to touch me and it's not because
>   anyone hurt me—it's just because
>   sex isn't something I'm interested*

in. But I could write poems
about love
forever.

People have sex without
love all the time. You
should be able to have
love without
sex.

    You think so?

If somebody says you
can't, then I'll turn them
to stone. How's that?

    It's a plan, Stan.

We sit shoulder to shoulder

in the stacks
until the bell
rings.

I learn
ISAP isn't

the only
place to find
peace.

This time Coach Tinsley is waiting at the bus stop

and I don't see him until it's too late, until I'm already
panting to a stop after my sprint from Mr. Mattson's class.

We meet again! he jokes, and I try not to roll my eyes,
at least not where he can see. I keep my eye on the road
waiting for the bus to appear. One thing
about getting faster
is that I'm here earlier every day, more time
to wait, more time to be seen.

In the corner of my eye, the track team
is moving down the block toward the track,
and I think I see the tall figure of Jacob Wheeler
paused, watching the bus stop.

Coach sees him too. *Jacob tells me you used to run!*
I'm new, as you know. I had no idea . . .

He goes on, thinking he's giving me
this big pitch: they need more girls,
they need more 400-meter runners,
more girls for relay, just
more girls. I'm fast.
I seem in shape. Not much conditioning.
There's a meet in three weeks.
I could be part of a team, part of something,
I could get scouted for college . . .

But behind him the school doors are opening,
the sound of squeaking steel,
and the Colonel appears
in the sunlight like a shark fin
cutting above the waves.

153

I should have known
that today felt too
smooth.

What do you say? Coach Tinsley says, grinning,
stupid, oblivious. *Come meet the team next week.*
You know athletes get to skip class sometimes, right?

I can't look at him. I don't know if he is man
or wolf or just too young to know
what world he's walking in.

But the bus has come to save me
and I let it bear me away without giving
him an answer.

Another headline about a celebrity who DMed a teenager

They all blur together eventually: actors
singers, priests, presidents,
teachers, mentors, respected
members of society.

Everyone is always so surprised
when the fleece comes off,
when the wolf is unsheathed:

everyone clutches
their pearls

meanwhile
in the shadows
there are always girls
and boys
who heard the howls

when everybody else
was too busy clapping
or saying
amen.

Texts with Deja

Deja: Can I ask you a question?

Alicia: I might not have an answer, but sure

Deja: What does it feel like to want sex? Like . . . sexual attraction.
Desire. What's that like?

Alicia: ooh awkward

Deja: 😐

Alicia: ok fine. I mean, it's hard to describe. It's just . . . there.
Somewhere between fire and ache. Like your skin is hungry
for that person. Like your body is alive, but more than just your
heart beating. Like it's directing your brain to seek out touch.
Idk. Does that make sense?

Deja: NOPE

Alicia: welp

Deja: My friends always say that I just haven't met the right person,
and when I do I'll feel different about sex and attraction. But I
really don't think so.

Alicia: I feel like you probably know yourself better than anybody
else does.

Deja: My sister said, "Just wait, you feel like this now, but one day
you'll bloom like a sunflower." But I already feel like a sunflower.
I'm open, golden, glowing.

Alicia: I hate when people act like who you are is a phase.

Deja: Why do people find a way to think something is wrong with
a girl no matter what? One minute we're not supposed to be
having sex, but as soon as a girl doesn't want to have sex with

155

ANYBODY, something's wrong with that too? "Oh you're secretly gay." Or, with Black girls, "Oh your standards are too high."

Alicia: Idk, I still think virgins have the easiest time. Comparatively speaking.

Deja: Nah. No one has the easiest time, see? It's like a kaleidoscope duct-taped to a sniper rifle. Everything so pretty until the crosshairs turn on.

Alicia: Hm true. The rules always change

Deja: Who makes the rules? Let's beat their ass

Alicia: Arthur-fist.gif

More texts with Deja

Deja: btw Isis said she saw you talking to Coach Tinsley. You thinking of running again . . . ? 👀

Alicia: I don't have time for extracurriculars

Deja: What, because of work? Colleges don't care about Meat Palace, girl!

Alicia: I don't care about colleges, so the feeling is mutual

Deja: You can't work at Meat Palace your whole life

Alicia: Why not

Deja: The better question is WHY. What are you hiding from?

Things I don't tell Deja

My whole life is how it feels
when you get your purse stolen.

You don't have anything of value anymore.
You don't have a way to prove who you are
because your ID is gone. Everything
feels empty. You're afraid to care

about anything too much
because what if
it just gets
stolen
again?

My mother pretends everything is normal

and still hasn't acknowledged the text I sent her
about waiting up. She moves around the kitchen
making dinner, and I watch her from the doorway
before she notices I'm home. Something about her
looks different, some subtle adjustment to her shoulders.

I examine her for evidence of love, for traces
of a new man who has straightened her spine.
When her eyes catch mine, she smiles.

Hey Turtle, I'm glad to see you, she says, and points
at all the dishes that need doing.
She hasn't called me Turtle
for what feels like a lifetime.

Have you asked David? I ask, already
pushing up my sleeves.

He's not here, she says.
Just us.

I almost tell her.

We're side by side and the light is low
and somehow with both of us in shadow

it seems like it might be easier here to say
the words that live on the tip of my tongue:

Adam hurt me and then the Colonel hurt me
and now I've been hurting me
and I need you to help me make it stop

But my brain is a nest of hypotheticals
and all I can think about is the questions
she would ask:

Why was I alone with either
of these men, what was I wearing,
what did I say, how did I smile,
did I say no, or was I just silent,
because silence doesn't count

Plus as she hands me more dishes
to bury in soap, she seems relaxed,
her smile hasn't yet retreated
to the corners of the kitchen,

and this is the first time since she kicked
my father out that she has stayed
in the room beside me for more
than five minutes, and I can't bear
to be the thing that seizes her smile
with pliers and flings it into the dark—

I can't bear to be one more thing
in her life that didn't turn out
exactly as she'd hoped.

There's a blinking voicemail on the machine

and I delete it while she puts the leftovers away,
her back turned and oblivious.

I don't need to hear it before knowing it needs
to disappear. It is either my father
maybe calling on the way to Cincinnati,
bags packed, or it is my school
calling to express polite concern
about the girl with poison hair
and a poison mouth.

Neither message
is welcome
here.

MONDAY, DECEMBER 17
It's actually cold now and that means coats.

I pull out the red puffer coat I've worn
for the last two winters—it still fits,
but unlike last year, when my hair was still
light brown, the color of a rabbit,
now my head matches the coat.

I stare at myself in the mirror,
the way I look like a warning:
STOP
WRONG WAY
NO TRESPASSING

I am always thinking of myself
as a salamander

or a traffic signal
and never as a girl.

I wonder if any of Medusa's
snakes were red.

My mother tells me to wear a hat

but she's distracted. It's the kind of advice
she feels required to offer. My brother
is already gone, or maybe he's still here
but asleep in the basement. Neither
my mother nor I check. She offers

a ride to the bus stop but I say no.
She doesn't know I take public,
and she wouldn't understand
the way the school bus
feels like walking into the steel jaws
of an animal trap, the kind that snaps
the ankle, cuts through
to the bone. She doesn't understand

that I need an option of escape,
that a school bus driver
doesn't have to listen,
that there is no string to pull
when the air begins to thicken
in your lungs. I know what she would say:

Isn't that the point?
To get students to school
without letting them get off?

And I would say
Exactly

The cafeteria is always quiet on the first really cold day.

The last of autumn has leaked
out of everyone's bones
and left chilled waiting rooms,
everybody already thinking
about spring,

bitter about the puffy coats
that take up all the space
in the slender cells of lockers.

I scan the huddled masses for Geneva,
lower my eyes before I can find her.

I can feel people staring at me,
at the redness of my being.

Hair.
Coat.
Rage.

I feel myself starting to transform
in their eyes
from the slutty girl
to the scary girl

and that's okay
with me.

The announcement speaker crackles to life

and everyone jumps or shivers
like the sound of it was a defibrillator's
electrodes placed against our collective chest.

Principal Warren's voice addresses us:

There will be a special presentation today—

and everyone cheers, because a disrupted day
is a good day—

*as we introduce an interim faculty member
Dr. Kareem, who will be spending some time
with us at Marshall as she does research
for her university. If you see Dr. Kareem
in the halls please welcome her warmly*

but no one really hears or cares
no one has any intention of being warm
no one has any intention of doing anything
but what they had already decided to do:

sleep during Dr. Kareem's presentation.
Myself included.

Text from a random at 9am

Him: I know it's early but are you free?
Alicia: I'm at school
Him: Don't you get a lunch break?
Alicia: I can't leave during break
Him: Maybe you can sneak out?

It has never occurred to me to skip school

and I stare at my phone as the bell rings,
new wells being dug beneath me,
caves I have yet to spelunk.

There are two security guards at Marshall
and probably a dozen doors.
Surely people skip all the time.

His name is Randy
and I think I gave him my number
at the bus stop.

His face swims
in my memory,
blurred with other
faces, other days.

He hasn't seen me naked
but wants to.

This is the part
where I am supposed to feel wary
about what kind of guy
wants to pick up a girl
for sex at 9am.

This is the part
where survival instincts
are supposed to rise like
back-of-neck hairs.

This is the part
where I'm supposed to love

myself enough to see
that he doesn't care
about me or my life.

But I don't.
I text him back
Okay

Deja texts me as I'm dropping my books off

Deja: Have you seen the Dr. Kareem lady yet?

Alicia: No is she here already?

Deja: Yeah me and Isis just met her in the hallway outside 1st. She
looks like a freakin supermodel!

Alicia: Meaning she looks hungry?

Deja: omg shut up. Body-shaming skinny folks is still body-shaming!

Alicia: My apologies to all the rich and famous supermodels

Deja: Anyway! You have to sit with me and Isis during the
presentation. Dr. Kareem said she's starting some type of group
for women at Marshall. Maybe she'll pick us!

Alicia: Oh . . . I wasn't going to go actually

Deja: wtf do you mean you weren't going to go? The whole school
has to go

Alicia: . . .

Deja: Even ISAP. So forget about it. See you there. Third row.

Maybe Deja is divine intervention.

Maybe the Randy dude is a serial killer.
Maybe when I don't answer his text
asking where to pick me up

he goes on a rampage
and drives off a cliff.

Maybe I dodged a bullet.
Or maybe not.

Either way, I guess I'm going
to this stupid presentation
where Deja and Isis
will sit on either side of me
like a chaperone sandwich.

My mother texts me as I'm walking into the auditorium

and the pit in my stomach deepens.

I need to talk to you when you get home, she says.

I have to work, I text back.

PHONES AWAY, a twelfth-grade teacher barks. He's talking to
      someone else
but not for long.

I'll be home waiting for you, my mother says.

Is someone dead?

No is all she says.

I almost wish someone were,
so I would know what to expect:
a corpse, and not the gray castle
of possibilities that my brain
begins to build.

Dr. Kareem isn't skinny but she does look like a supermodel.

She's the kind of person who carries a torch in her face.
Every smile is electric, every gesture
of her black-polished fingers
like free birds.

She stands on the stage and speaks boldly
into the mic and you can tell she's used to it,
to speaking out into a dark room,
because it's like the mic isn't there at all,

no *can you hear me now* jokes
no *is this thing on.*
It *is* on
and so is she

and I'm suddenly very glad
I didn't sneak out through
a non-emergency exit
into the car of a man named Randy.

I am suddenly very glad
I am here in this school
for once

because the Colonel is sitting on the far side
with Ms. Balwick and Mrs. Fisher, listening
to every word when Dr. Kareem says straight
into the mic:

Everyone thinks they know how to solve
the problem of girls,

girls who are so-called problems, but rarely
does someone ask those girls how
they'd like to be solved,
or if they see themselves as a problem
or a reaction.

Dr. Kareem says she's going to choose a group of girls

from all walks of life
whatever that means

to join her in the music room
after winter break.
The group will meet on Fridays,
when they will be excused

from class to take part in her study
where she listens to the girls talk

about their lives and their challenges
and what inspires them.

I know right then she is not going to pick
a girl like me. Why would she choose

someone who has only ever inspired
a faceless classmate to carve

Alicia Rivers is a dyke hoe
into the face of a desk?

Ms. Gladstone's class is full of talk

after Dr. Kareem's presentation: the girls
are excited about a woman like Dr. Kareem
being interested in their lives
and the boys are jealous that they
for once
had to listen to something
that didn't place them
at the center.

I don't know why we all even had to go,
says Greg Wayne. *It was all about*
girls.

The same reason, says Audrey,
that the whole school has to go to the pep rally
for your stupid football games
that you guys never win.

And even though she called me a skank
I still find my mouth
curving into a smiling snarl.

At the end of the day, Geneva is at my locker,

and all my muscles that were poised to sprint
for the bus stop suddenly slacken into syrup
rolling slowly from the maple. I stand apart, staring

and she sees me then, a smile radiating from her face
like sun bouncing off water. It catches me, holds me
still. *What are you doing after school?* she says.

I have to work.

Do you walk? I think I saw you walking
last week.

Sometimes.

Can I walk with you?

I don't know if I actually say
yes. I must, because she smiles
again, and then moves slightly
to the side, a signal: We can go
now.

We go.
We walk.
I don't notice
the cold.

Walking conversation with Geneva

Geneva: *How long have you worked at Meat Palace?*
Alicia: *Two years.*
Geneva: *Do you like it?*
Alicia: *Absolutely not. But the people are cool sometimes.*
Geneva: *I think that was the longest string of words I've ever heard*
from your mouth.
Alicia:
Geneva: *Except when I've heard you cussing out Mrs. Fisher.*
We laugh.
Geneva: *Why does she hate you?*
Alicia: *I don't know.*
Geneva: *I think there are certain people that are like security sensors*
and when a bag goes through that sets them off, they freak out.
Alicia: *Am I the sensor or the bag?*

Geneva: I think you set Mrs. Fisher off, is what I'm saying. Something
   about you sets her off.
Alicia: . . . so I'm the bag.
Geneva: I mean, I think you're carrying a lot. So yeah.

Things I learn about Geneva on the way to Meat Palace: Part 1

- She says "bagel" like "BAG-el"
- She says "bag" like "bayeg"
- She does not mind the cold
- She does not eat fast food
- She's never been to Pakistan, where her dad was from, but she wants to
- She wants a Godzilla tattoo
- She has a cat named Morpheus
- She moved here with her mom to be with her grandmother, who has cancer
- Marshall is not as bad as her old school
  - but there were no Pakistani girls there (or here) and it's a special kind of lonely
- She used to play the clarinet
- She had her first girlfriend when she was thirteen

Things I learn about Geneva on the way to Meat Palace: Part 2

She has a way of making you feel
seen. She only has two eyes
like anyone else but the things

she says make it seem like her body
is covered in eyes, like her mouth
her hands
her feet

are eyes of their own
and when she speaks
when she touches
when she walks

she is seeing
everything
seeing me,
and drinking it
all in.

Things I learn about me on the way to Meat Palace: Part 1

There is a flock of birds that live
inside my rib cage
and when Geneva Dhaliwal
speaks, all their wings
fill with air
and make circles
in the sky
of my body

Things I learn about me on the way to Meat Palace: Part 2

I am

    halfway

in love
with a
girl named
Geneva Dhaliwal

    already.

Mariah the misanthrope quit.

I walk into drive-thru thinking I will tell her
about the walk with the girl with a name
that sounds like
    a superhero
    a wildflower
    a famous scientist
    a magic spell
but instead of Mariah it is Debbie
who has worked at Meat Palace since she was sixteen
and whose fingers twist like curly fries
from arthritis.

She smiles silently, pointing at the headphones
to indicate she's currently taking an order,
as if I can't hear their voice like a drum major
echoing out: *Gimme a . . .*

I turn away, pretend to check the stock of sauce
in the lobby but really I'm looking out the front

window to see if I can still glimpse the form
of Geneva walking back toward school
alone, but she's already
gone.

I think of Geneva the entire way home,

like her presence is a bottle
of sunshine I sip from in the gloom of night.

The bottle only goes empty when I walk in
and find my mother sitting in the kitchen,
waiting. Her text has been looming
on the horizon of my mind. *No one is dead,*
I remind myself,
but that still seems like the best-case
scenario. Her face is flat.

I sit down across from her and she presses
her hands against the table, mouth pinched.

She takes a deep breath and I just know
that my whole shadowed life is about to spill
out of her mouth and onto the floor
between us.

She opens her lips:

*I think there's something wrong
with your brother,* she says,

and she's so serious when she says it
her eyes so blue
that it takes a moment for the words

to catch up to the fearful hope
in my head.

We just look at each other, and when
I am finally able to speak
all I can think to say is
No shit, Mom.
No shit.

David isn't home.

Of course.
He is an apple

on a branch
that took a knife

to itself.

He falls far
from the place
he grew

and calls himself
a pear
instead.

If David's a pear then I'm a lemon.

All my thoughts are sour acid.
I sit in my room with my back
against the door and listen
to my mother's voice drifting
in, talking to her mother:

I was worried about David
but now something
has gotten into Alicia.
I feel like I'm fucking
this all up, Mom, how
am I supposed to fix
something I didn't
break

and my chest squeezes
with guilt, hearing
the tears in her voice,
but I can't make myself
open the door and go
to her arms.

Sometimes I think about the little things

that when shoved into the same frame
grow enormous.

The day in Kroger with Adam,
my dad ignoring the staring cashier,
my mom too worried about the text
my dad was checking on his phone
to notice the flush in my cheeks.

The day at the optometrist
getting glasses I would never wear.
The man, my dad's age, who slipped
the spectacles onto my face and adjusted
their arms over my ears, letting his fingers
trail against my cheek, looking

through the crystal lens and deep
into my eyes. My stomach was in knots,
my mouth sewed shut. I kept looking
at my parents but neither of them
seemed to notice and it only made the pit
in my stomach dig deeper, feeling
visible and invisible at the same time.

The boy, Donald, at church whose mother
was a meteorologist on the local news.
The way he would scrutinize my outfit
every Sunday, right around the time
my boobs were coming in. His eyes
like shears, cutting everything off,
including skin. *Going to need new shirts*
soon, Alicia. Those aren't going to fit
for long. You're going to swell up
all over soon and the youth minister
would pretend Donald was making fat jokes
which would have been fucked up enough
but this was something else.

For as long as I can remember
I have been afraid of my body
as it is,
but also
afraid of what
it will inevitably
become,
and whose.

I read an article about mass shootings

and how when a person survives one
　　in a movie theater perhaps
they may never go to the movies again.

The wide dark,
the silver glow,
only the narrow aisles
for cover . . .

it's all too much.

Sites of trauma.

And I think that school
has obviously become
a site of trauma for me

but so has Kroger
and the park
and sometimes
the bus

even though it is also
a vessel of freedom.

But the thing that all
these sites have in common
　　is my body,
and I wonder
sometimes
how you avoid a site
of trauma when the site
is your own self

and I think the answer is
you stop thinking of the body
    as yours
and maybe that makes it
easier to walk
inside it.

I don't have Geneva's phone number

but I know her Instagram now, and in the cave
of my room I scroll
and scroll

through every smile
every burrito
every Boomerang

by the time morning
leaks through my window
I think I know her
life by heart.

Somehow I end up looking at Blake,

pictures of her golden legs
pictures of her golden life

I think there must be a line
too fine to see—
one that separates
good girls
and bad ones.

Sometimes my life feels like climate change,
everything that's wrong
too massive to fully comprehend,
crushing and hot
and inescapable.

Looking at Blake is like looking
at an ice cap that won't melt
a polar bear that never goes extinct.

Maybe I could be that cold
if it meant I would
survive.

Text with Deja interrupts the Blake rabbit hole

Deja: I think I'm going to quit debate team. I'm so sick of Clay.

Alicia: His smirk makes me feel stabby and I've never even had
class with him. I don't blame you.

Deja: It's just, I was there first, you know? It was fine before
Mr. Hudson took over.

Alicia: Mr. Hudson is dopey. He's like that guy who wasn't cool in
high school and so he tries to side with the cool kids now like it
will make him one of them.

Deja: Who's cool? CLAY?

Alicia: Clay Bevin, Blake Felipe, all of them. They know everyone's
jealous of them (including Mr. Hudson) and they love it.

Deja: lmfao I don't know who this *everyone* you speak of is,
but there's nobody on this earth I'm jealous of except maybe
Normani. Maybe.

Alicia: You know what I mean. Popular kids, their big golden circles.

Deja: Psh their circles aren't the only circles.

Deja has a theory

This is the first time she sends me a voice note, and I mistake
it for an accident at first—a brief scuffle before her voice
wheels out of my phone's speaker:

Too much to text so hear me out. What you said about circles has me
   thinking.
I think there is a big circle we're all supposed to stay at the middle of—
not a circle, actually. There's a heart *that claims to love us*
and we are supposed to exist at its center, right? As long as we stay

at the center, we are loved. People like Blake and Clay
are popular the way a mirage in the desert offers water.
They never stray from the center, and are loved
for it.

But lately I've been feeling off-balance.
And I realize the more I learn about
myself, the farther from that center I am
and even though it means I am not like Blake
or Clay, the farther from that center I get
the freer I feel. Does that make sense?

That the farther you get from the thing
that claims to love you as long as you obey
its rules, the happier
you will be?

I don't want to answer for myself—
not yet—so I send her a voice note
back:

What rules are you breaking?

When she answers back, she's laughing:

180

Alicia, I think I'm starting to realize
that my whole self is a broken rule.

Up late thinking of Sarah

like a never-ending game of solitaire
or, more accurately,
Jenga:

my years as her best friend
a wobbling tower
as I pull and slide
each wooden memory.

Those should be our people,
she said.

Words like *popular* and *cool kids*
golden boy/girl
perfect perfect perfect—

all the things and lives
we were supposed to be jealous of.

What about Blake sparks envy?
Of all the girls at Marshall
why was she sticky enough
to catch the fly of my eye?

I think again of pennies
dropping into purses—
the thing I'm not smart enough
to see swims into view once more.

It still doesn't quite
click.

All I know is that Sarah always
had her eye on the throne
and maybe that's part of why
when I fell short
I fell so, so far.

Up late(r) thinking of freedom,

and what Deja said about finding it
far from the center of an unloving heart.

First my skin and then my mind remembers
Ray Rangeland, him whispering across the front
seat: *When do you feel the most free?*

Running, still.

If Blake is at the center of that circle-heart,
I am running for the perimeter, but

I haven't bumped into that free feeling
Deja talks about—not since Renée
in a cabin surrounded by the songs
of crickets. Although maybe my fingers
skimmed its edge that night with Ray.

Deja talked about kaleidoscopes and rifles—
maybe I've been looking at this all wrong.

Freedom not just the doing, but the being.
Sometimes when someone's tongue
is in my mouth, my eyes are open
looking for the horizon.

It's three in the morning and I run
my tongue across my own smooth teeth.

WEDNESDAY, DECEMBER 19

I forgot about Dr. Kareem until I almost tripped her.

Walking down the hall, my eyes on my shoes,
and suddenly there was another pair
of shoes in my field of vision,
and they were stumbling,
and my arm shot out
and steadied the person
they belonged to, and when
I looked up, it was Dr. Kareem
who had also been looking down,
reading a yellow-paged notebook
full of red-inked chicken scratch.

We stared at each other, surprised
to find someone's universe
overlapping with our own,
and then she smiled, a faint
smile of something like
recognition.

Thank you, she said. *Alicia, I think?*

How do you know my name?

I'm learning lots of people's names, she said.

Some people call me Red, I said.
(And silently: *among other things*)

And she said, *What do you
call you?*

And I said, *Alicia, I guess.*

And she said, *Then I will call you
Alicia.*

Texts with Deja

Alicia: I met Dr. Kareem
Deja: Isn't she dope?
Alicia: She smells like honey
Deja: That's something you say about someone you have a crush on

Sometimes you get too comfortable.

I have gotten used to secrets
and keeping them.

With Deja I have been
loosening my lips.

I do not have a crush
on Dr. Kareem
but with Deja
I have gotten comfortable

saying what I think
without wondering
how it's going to sound
and now she's heard.

Texts with Deja two minutes later

Deja: I hope that didn't come off homophobic. I didn't mean it like that. I just meant she kind of has that effect on people. I'm not even gay and she gives me butterflies

Alicia: Oh okay

Deja: I know you like girls, Alicia. I don't care. So does Amanda. She's a lesbian-lesbian though. No boys at all.

Alicia: Oh

Deja: I don't care, okay? Don't be weird.

Alicia: Okay

Deja: You're being weird

Alicia: I am?

Deja: Please relax lol

I actually do relax.

It's a strange feeling, especially
here at school. So relaxed
I fall asleep in Mrs. Fisher's class.

Although maybe that's because
I didn't sleep last night.

Either way, she sends me
to ISAP. Home
away from home.

I pass my locker on the way,

and almost miss the corner of paper
sticking out, blue ink
visible through the fold.

It's like smoke in the distance,
the silent roar of a far-off
forest fire burning
its way forward.

My whole life is already ablaze,
I don't want to look
but I do—

*We should talk—
I know your secret.*

and all I can do is think
Jesus, kid, which one?

Mr. West opens the door and sees me.

Sighs.
Points to
a desk.

Says, *One day*
I'm going
to get tired
of seeing
you in here
and I'm going
to show up
at your house
and talk
to your parents

and something
like a cringe
must wound

my face because
he frowns
shakes his head
and says
*but it won't
be today.*

Sometimes I wonder what normal secrets are like

the kind that don't compel anonymous
blue pens to harass you via locker door:

A boyfriend your parents
don't like.

A C+ in calculus.

A joint smoked
behind the garage.

A window snuck
out of for a kiss.

A car borrowed
for a summer joyride,
returned silently
to the garage.

Secrets that,
if discovered,
would merely dent
the fender

not rend the machine
into pieces of shattered
metal.

Ms. Gladstone keeps me after class.

Her eyes are worried jewels
behind museum glass.
I see myself reflected
above the half frown.

I wanted to tell you today,
she says, *so you're not taken
by surprise.*

Does she feel the pit
in my stomach, dropping
and dropping?

*Dr. Kareem asked the faculty
for recommendations
on girls to be included
in her study.
I told her I thought
you should be one of the twelve.*

I say nothing and she keeps
talking:

*I know you're having a tough year
but I think you have a lot to say
and could contribute
something important
to the group.*

She asks if that's okay
and I barely stop myself

from saying *Does it matter?*
because it's already done.
But as pissed as I am
I keep it to myself

because Ms. Gladstone
isn't Mrs. Fisher and I think
she means well, even if
she has just decided
to put the salamander of my life
under the glass of a microscope.

Geneva's coming toward me after school and I run.

I spent half the night scrolling through her smile,
                    but right now I need to feel the burn of my lungs
to remind myself that I may not have control
                              over anything else in my life, but I can
always make the choice to run.

I see Coach Tinsley under an umbrella watching from the track

but I keep going. I don't wait
for the bus, I don't wait
for the rain to stop.

I run all the way to Meat Palace
and don't stop until
I'm in the break room,
chest heaving, legs shaking.

My clothes are soaking wet,
a puddle growing slowly
around me.

Stephanie appears
*You know you don't
work today, right?
It's Wednesday.*

And she's right,
but I sit in the break room
for a half hour anyway
listening to the rain.

Any port
in a storm.

Debbie comes to slice the beef.

I can smell the cigarette smoke drifting off her clothes
from where I sit three feet away. She loads
the big hunk of beef onto the slicer
and runs it expertly, steam rising,
the thin layers of meat falling
into the stainless steel.

She sees me watching and smiles.
*I could do it in my sleep.
I'm better at slicing beef
than I am anything else.*

*I've sliced more beef
than I have licked envelopes*

than I have picked flowers
than I have blown out birthday candles.

I've given this place a lot of years
and one finger,

and she holds up the stump,
wiggles the remaining digits
around it. I never noticed

until now. *That happened*
here? I ask, and she nods.
Right where I'm standing.

Sometimes I still feel it—
I lost a part of myself
but we still remember each other.

She's talking about her finger
but after she leaves with the beef
I sit and cry.

I wait until the rain stops

then walk home. There are three texts
on my phone that I've been avoiding:

Mom: Would you be interested in talking to another therapist? Not
   about the divorce but just about . . . you?
Random: Free tonight?
Deja: Isis is thinking about quitting dance and running track. They
   need more girls. She doesn't wanna do it alone tho. Would you
   do it if she did?

Everybody has questions
and I have no answers.

When I text Deja back I ignore her question and ask my own

Alicia: If I knew something about someone, something bad, would
you want to know

Deja: Someone I know?

Alicia: Kinda

Deja: Someone at school?

Alicia: Kinda

Deja: Is there a serial killer in your physics class or something

Alicia: No

Deja: Are there monsters among us?

Alicia: Yeah, me

Deja: lol plz

Weed and cats.

I smell Justin before I see him,
although he's just putting on
his coat to leave—maybe he's
been waiting for the rain too.

He ignores me, steps outside,
my brother close behind, watching
him cross the lawn.

Are you gay? I ask
when it's just me and David.
Do you like him?

You're so fucking stupid,
he says. *Why, do you want
to fuck* him *too?*

It feels like a black hole
has opened in my throat
as I realize the things
people say about me
have reached my brother's
ears, and he would rather

spit it all back at me
than choose not
to hear.

I almost tell him the truth.

He's my big brother.

In the movies,
the father
the brother
the uncles
(except the dirty one)
all combine to form
a human umbrella
a sword
for the girl child.

It's patriarchal,
I know.
It implies
that girls

can't take care of ourselves
and that women
won't,

but it's one stereotype
I sometimes wish
were true in my life:

to have men
in your life
who know
that the battle
we face against
men who are
wolves can only
be won
with the help
of men
who are not.

My brother hasn't seen me cry

since we were little kids. I'm not much
of a crier, and besides, I already
cried at work, and twice
in one day just seems excessive.

Lately all my tears
have transformed
from blue to red,

so even though my brother's
words are a dagger
in my heart, I don't cry.

Instead it all turns to rage
and I scream at him
in this empty house,

so loud my throat
feels like broken glass

so loud his eyes
go wide,

like a trespasser who mistook
a ghost
for a sheet.

I scream at him
until he goes to his room,
closes the door
against my magnificent
fury, and I stand at it
screaming
until I run out
of words.

Texts with Deja

Deja: You know you have read notifications on.
Alicia: ?
Deja: So when I ask you stuff and you don't respond I see you've
read it and are just ignoring me
Alicia: Not ignoring. Considering.
Deja: Yeah yeah well CONSIDER telling me why you don't wanna
run track
Alicia: I told you
Deja: It ain't about your schedule. What I look like, BooBoo the fool?

Alicia: I'm not acquainted with BooBoo.

Deja: lol You get on my nerves

Alicia: ☺

Up late thinking about Medusa

I'm starting to realize
that a woman doesn't get that mad

> so mad that her hair turns to snakes
> so mad that her rage turns blood to boulder
> so mad that she withdraws into a cave
> > and dares the world to follow

all on her own.

I realize I've been thinking
of myself as a ghost
but I've been comparing
myself to the wrong
kind of monster.

THURSDAY, DECEMBER 20
It's Thursday and I'm embarrassed of my butterflies.

They're going to announce Dr. Kareem's girl group
in homeroom. It feels stupid to be nervous
about something I don't even want.

(Do I?)
The butterflies in my stomach
feel more like maggots,
inching up my esophagus.
Somehow thinking of it

as butterflies
feels like thinking
I deserve to be chosen—

the maggots feel more appropriate,
swimming through the rot of me.

Still, when Ms. Gladstone reads
the list of twelve girls—
three from each grade—
I see the flutter of the smile
on her lips

and think maybe in the crawl
and creep of my maggots
she sees a flash of green,
like a caterpillar
instead.

The list

Freshmen
I don't know any of these girls
I don't know any of these girls
I don't know any of these girls

Sophomores
I don't know any of these girls
Tierra Pryor (she runs track)
I don't know any of these girls

Juniors
Prya Farooqi
Alicia Rivers
Deja Duvall (thank god)

Seniors
Lena Herman (also runs track)
Eugenia De León
Blake Felipe (of course)

A lot of girls are bummed out that they weren't chosen

but I can't help but think we are all excited
about something we have no name for.

We have no idea what we are getting into
with Dr. Kareem, only that we will be allowed
to miss class once a week.

Maybe that's enough for us all.
(Since when do I say *we* and *us*?)

Ms. Gladstone makes eyes at me,

wanting me to be happy about this thing
that will occasionally free me from class.

Maybe she thinks that's the only reason
I would want to do it.

What I'm happy about is that next week is winter break,
that I won't see the Colonel

or Mrs. Fisher, or even ISAP
until after the new year.

My mind is busy on the way to art
until I reach the place in the hall

that always brings me back to Earth,
as if the ground itself grows hot.

But today the sight of the Colonel's door
plunges me not into fire, but ice.

The door is closed again, and that only
means one thing.

Is there a word for this feeling?

I am an emotional flashbang.

I am a blank stare.

I am a well of dread.

I am a tongue of fire.

But mostly
I am gray
as guilty stone

because the sight
of that door
closed

just makes me relieved
that I'm not
behind it.

But . . .

Someone is.

Someone is.

Someone

is.

    Someone
        is.

        Someone
          is.

I can't paint anything in studio.

I pick up the brush
but it feels like the fire
that has been keeping
me alive has smoldered.

All I can do is dip the brush
in white paint,
make circles
and circles
and circles,
everything invisible
and happening
over and over again.

When Geneva appears
by my side she doesn't speak.

She rests her hand
on my shoulder
and leaves it there
while the white circles
go on
and on.

Ms. Gupta makes Geneva go back to her seat
and part of me is relieved because the warmth of her hand
on my shoulder was like a living thing,
and the way that Geneva seems
to be made of eyes, seeing everything,
makes me feel that if left there long enough

her hand would become
X-ray
stethoscope
thermometer

seeing and sensing
the bones
the breath
the fever

of every secret
hidden in the wound
that is my body.

But Ms. Gupta can't keep Geneva from walking with me after class

and I'm relieved about that too,
the way having her by my side

as we pass the Colonel's class
door now open
makes me feel safer
like a ship sheltered
by a lighthouse
while passing through
that dark water.

I know we don't know each other very well,
she says, *but Sunday is my birthday.*

I'm having a sleepover.
You should come.

And then she's
gone.

We're too old for sleepovers.

I haven't been to one since I was ten,
and I picture Disney movies
and popcorn
and someone's mother
with crossed arms
calling down the stairs
that 9pm is too late.

And right now
standing beside my locker
alone, I still picture Disney
movies, but I also
picture Geneva, beside me
on the couch

in a room lit only
by the television.

Our bare arms turn silver
as they move
closer and closer
to touching.

I'm supposed to work the day of the sleepover.

The plan was to work
all through winter break.
But maybe
just maybe
I will tell Terry
I have
strep throat.

I can't go to a sleepover.

I'm sixteen years old.
I don't even know Geneva.
I don't know any of her friends.
I don't even know how old she will be.
I don't know why she invited me.
But I do know that I can't stop
writing her name along the edge
of my favorite notebook.

Random thoughts about Debbie's finger

I've heard you can reattach
the thing that's been severed
but only if you find it in time
before rot sets in

and I wonder
if it's the same
with souls:

if you have a finite
amount of time
to find the thing
you've lost
before
you are forever
soulless.

Reattachment

One time at Sarah's house
her brother left to drive
his new girlfriend home
and all Sarah's mom did
was rag on the girl, Gina,
because so-and-so's mother's
coworker saw her going
into Planned Parenthood last year

and I feel like this city
is too big to be this small

but I guess it's not big enough
to contain something as massive
as Gina walking through
that black-tinted door.

I've lost count of all the things
that Sarah could condemn me for
so when I think about Debbie's finger
and my dirty soul
I also think about hymens
and whether when you're a born-again
Christian, if that can be restored too,

and I almost laugh to imagine Sarah
torn between which she loves more:
the Word of God,
or hating me.

My brother actually speaks

when I walk in the house, looking up
from his pizza rolls to say
I saw Sarah today.

It's like I conjured her.

There she is:

at the sink washing mud
off her church shoes

in the corner playing hide-
and-seek

in the mirror looking at new
braces.

I'm pretty sure it was her anyway,
he says. *I almost forgot*
what she looked like
and I just shrug, but inside
I think

I haven't.

FRIDAY, DECEMBER 21
"Have you ever told her how you feel?"

"Maybe she doesn't know she hurt your feelings."
I'm eavesdropping on the bus:
two college students sitting close,
young men with backpacks
on their laps.

She wouldn't care, says his friend.
All she cares about is her fucking piano.

And I don't know who they're talking about
or who this piano-loving person is

but I think I agree with the dude:
some people are so focused
on the things that are important to them
that your wounds are insignificant.

Maybe it doesn't mean that they're evil,
but it doesn't mean you're not bleeding.

Fantasy vs. reality

FANTASY

Walking into school
and finding the halls empty.

The track team girls
who graduated last year
are back.

The Colonel's classroom
is empty, boarded up.

Geneva is at my locker
and she's insisting
I come to her sleepover.

                                          REALITY

                                    I walk into school
                              and the halls are full
                    of the same eyes and mouths.

                              The track team seniors
                                    are still gone.

                        The Colonel's door is open,
                        and when I pass it for
                        art studio, I can hear him
                              inside humming.

                        Geneva is at my locker
                              and she is insisting
                        I come to her sleepover.

I'm so happy to see her

that my heart doesn't even clench
when it sees the white paper
sticking out of my locker.

I crumple it into the trash
without looking—at this point
I can tell that someone
is trying to get my attention

but I still refuse to look.

It's running weather

I don't know why
the gray sky

calls to me,
but it does.

It's cold. The track
team will be inside

doing laps, and so
when the bell rings

I make my way out
to the track, alone,

grateful for the stillness,
the company of silent pigeons.

I'm wearing khakis, as usual,
but I drop my backpack

by the gate
and begin.

My head may be a mess

but my legs work just fine.

Running on the track feels
different than sidewalk,
than hallway. The way
the path curves
is like déjà vu:

I have been here before
but the memories feel
like looking at something
through water:
wavering, blurred.

It becomes clearer
as I run, my lungs starting
to squeeze.

It's not just because I'm tired.
I feel as nervous as I would
if there were runners before
and behind, an actual race
and not just a foray into the cold.

I'm competing against nothing,
pushing against nothing
except the wolf in my mind

that stands between me
and everything I call mine.

Voices ruin everything.

I hear them coming, the echo of laughter
off the tan bricks darkened
by rain. The track team
is coming out after all, led by Coach Tinsley
carrying his clipboard, his whistle.

I'm almost to the finish line
but veer off, grab my backpack.
I hear my name in someone's mouth
but don't look back, just head
for the gate that will take me toward Chestnut.

Jacob Wheeler tries to catch up
but he's not made for sprints
he can't fly
the way I used to.

I make the track disappear
behind me, try not to think
about how I must look
to them:

roach skittering out of the light
rabbit scurrying for the bush
ghost sinking into the floor
a face lost in a nest of snakes

Teenage bumper stickers that no one believes

There's an assortment of things people say
that remind me of bumper stickers
stuck on the back of cars to convince people
they believe them, but no one does:

Who cares what other people think!

As long as you love yourself that's what matters!

Time heals all wounds!

Everyone cares what other people think
even if it's small, the size of a hangnail

Loving yourself is more complicated than algebra and physics
and I'm failing those things already

And that last one is just
bullshit

SUNDAY, DECEMBER 23
I tell my mother I'm going to a sleepover

and she doesn't even ask whose.
She assumes it's Sarah
and I let her. She thinks
my former life still exists
and I don't have the heart
to tell her that the person
she thinks is her daughter
has slowly gone extinct.

Texts with Deja on the bus

Deja: you remember what I told you in the library?

Alicia: wanting to turn people to stone?

Deja: kinda. What I said about not wanting to have sex

Alicia: yeah

Deja: I'm pretty sure it's not because I'm not ready. I think it's because I'm something else.

Alicia: like what?

Deja: I googled asexual and I think that's me. do you think that's weird?

Alicia: being asexual?

Deja: yeah

Alicia: do *you* think it's weird?

Deja: no.

Alicia: then no

Deja: I still like boys. I still love boys.

Alicia: you just don't want to have sex with them

Deja: right

Deja: so that's it? I'm just . . . asexual

Alicia: I mean, Ace sounds really cool tbh

More texts with Deja

Deja: rant incoming!!!

Alicia: lay it on me

Deja: I was sitting here zoning out while our pastor talks and you know what's some bullshit? Imagining how people are going to act if I tell them I'm asexual. Like, as a Black girl I REALLY can't win because on one tip, people make out Black girls to be TOO sexy, like everything we do is sex, even when we're just living life and wearing sneakers and eating Cheetos or whatever. So like, me being asexual, people will say YOU CAN'T BE ASEXUAL, YOU'RE TOO SEXY or whatever. But on the other tip, books and movies always cast the Black girl as the "friend" who never has a boyfriend and shit, like nobody wants us, so if I say I'm asexual, people will be like OH YOU'RE PLAYING INTO A STEREOTYPE OF BLACK GIRLS AS UNDESIRABLE. Like, I'm damned if I do, damned if I don't, and I just want to live my life and wear sneakers and eat Cheetos.

Alicia: You deserve all the Cheetos in the world.

Deja: Thank you. Yes, I do.

Alicia: Don't take this the wrong way, but church . . . kinda sucks. All that *purer than thou* bullshit.

Deja: Hold on now! lol But no, I feel that. I don't know if you've ever done Black church, but it does all the purity stuff too but . . . extra. I've had church ladies come up and tell me to pay special attention to the pastor's lectures on lust and temptation and I'm just sitting there like . . . this literally doesn't apply to me?

Alicia: To quote my ex-best friend, "Your body belongs to God first, and your husband second." 😒

Deja: I see why she's an ex. 🤮 It pisses me off because this all acts like sex is inevitable? Um, not for me! And it's not because the Virgin Mary is my bestie but because, like, this is who I am. It's not about being pure. I just wanna do what I wanna do.

Alicia: Which means NOT doing.

Deja: Let the church say amen! Also, you're a good friend.

Alicia:

Deja: I SEE that you read the message, Alicia. You can't pretend you don't see it when I give you love!

Alicia:

Deja: We are going to fight lol

Geneva's house is a normal house

Not big, not small.
Not dirty, not clean.
The curtains are new
but the carpet is old.
It is a house where a family
lives, and the walls
feel warm with conversation.

Her mother is painting the guest
room where Geneva's grandmother
will soon come to live, tells me
to make myself at home,
that the other girls
will be here soon.

I knew I would be the first
one here. I planned
to be late, but the bus
came on time
for once in its life
and delivered me three
blocks away. I couldn't
slow my feet, and here
I am, sitting on Geneva's couch
holding a glass of water

wondering how late
the bus runs in case
I need to escape.

She always smiles before she says something

that reveals the fact that she is made of eyes.
Her lip curls at the side. She holds her orange
calico cat on her lap, both of them gazing at me.

What, I ask.

You're not wearing khakis, she says.

So?

I thought you might wear them
as an excuse to leave for work
if you started to feel like
you don't want to be here.

I do want to be here.

For now, she says. *It's okay*
if you change your mind.

Then the doorbell rings

and her other friends are pouring
into the house, four girls
that don't go to Marshall.

Felicia, from her art group
Aida, from her art group
Michaela, a cousin
Parnisha, a neighbor

It is amazing to me
that Geneva has lived here

for five months
and has more friends
than I've ever had
in my entire life.

Not just friends
but sunrays
all smiling
all kind
all bearing gifts

And I hear my grandma's
voice in my head
Birds of a feather
and Mr. Mattson's voice
Like attracts like,

and I wonder
what kind of bird
what kind of element
am I, where
the kinds of things
I attract
are the friends

the people

who want

to hurt me.

All our songs

Michaela, the cousin, is the only one
who isn't a painter, but she
likes to sing, and when we've all
been introduced, she laughs
and says our names sound like a song

Felicia, Geneva, Aida
Michaela Parnisha,
Alicia

She sings our names one
after another, changing scales
until the sounds of who
we are blend into real music—
I can't tell where I end
and they begin.

Geneva's mom is a white woman named Genevieve

and it makes me smile to think about
all the men walking around the world
made sophisticated by the Junior
at the end of their signature,
a rubber stamp banged
down by a paternal hand,

and here is a woman
born in Minnesota
who decided that her daughter
would be named for her,

not so much a stamp
but a needle threaded
with two pieces of yarn,
woven together
but distinct.

When Geneva sits on the couch
Genevieve comes in
wearing paint-splattered coveralls
and bumps her daughter's elbow
with her hip. They share
the same smile
that reminds me of the rim
of a teacup, curved and warm.

When Genevieve disappears
to give the roomful of girls
privacy, she goes into her room
with the door closed,
starts a conversation
with someone on the phone.

In the living room, we're watching
a movie, but sometimes
when the scene is slow and quiet
I hear Genevieve in her room
laughing.

Geneva's dad was a chef

and he died when Geneva was eight.
That's old enough to remember.

There are pictures of him on the walls
on the way to the bathroom,
photos of him in the city
where he was born, Karachi,
Pakistan, where she told me he learned
to cook. I stop for a while to study
his face, the gifts he gave his daughter:

his wonderful almost-crooked nose
the playful arch of his eyebrows
the half-moon under each eye
that appeared when he smiled.

Geneva appears at my elbow
and that's when she tells me
about him, pointing to the photos
where he stands in toque
and apron, brandishing a knife
as if to stab his sous-chef,
his face comically devilish.

Cancer, she says.
*Sometimes it seems like
everyone has cancer.*

It does. Sometimes it seems
like everyone is suffering
from something, but I guess
it doesn't seem that way—
it's just the truth.

I was right about the Disney movies

and no one pretends to be too old.
I don't vote when the girls are deciding
what to watch but I'm glad when they pick
Moana over *Frozen*
and then later
Coco over *Frozen II.*

I don't participate,
but I am here,

and later still, when the dark
settles in, and everyone starts
to whisper, and secrets
drift out into the air,
I still don't participate

even as my back sinks
into the teal couch
that doesn't smell
like weed and cats.

I have so much I could say
especially as I hear
the inner worlds of Geneva's friends:

*My dad thinks he's like this business genius but sometimes he seems like
    he's twelve.*
*My cousin, she's always popping pills and everyone acts like it's not
    happening but it is.*
*This guy at my school is a senior and he's always trying to fuck
    freshmen.*

I decide to speak then, I say
That guy is a fucking wolf and someone needs to handle him

and everyone is surprised
especially me, because
who am I to talk about
what should be done about someone's wolf
when I can't even handle my own?

It's so much easier to talk about other people's problems

and together, me and Geneva
and these four girls I don't know
rip into the guys at each other's schools

There's a double standard for everything
and it's not just about who gets to sleep
around. It's everything. Boys get to be mad
about shit, they get to smash stuff
when they're pissed, they get to be full
of themselves. Even when they lose
they get to cry: when we cry
we're too emotional *and it's the reason*
we can't run the country;
when they cry because they lost
a football game everyone is like
"oh wow look that's so sweet
see men can be vulnerable"
I'm so tired of this shit

and all of Geneva's friends just nod
and say *so fucking true*

but Geneva catches my eye
in what's left of the light
and from the angle of her smile
I know she is seeing more
than I intended.

Like a prophecy becoming real before my eyes

the light of the television bathes our skin in silver.
Everyone is asleep on the floor, their breath
and the folds of blankets coming together like woven oceans.

Geneva is next to me on the couch and I'm staring
at the clock, at the 2am I'm always awake to see
but which somehow looks different here, where Geneva's
head slowly slides down to my shoulder.

It's not the slow nod of sleep, but a smooth decisive
readjustment, as if she decided that's where her temple
should rest, and made it so. My shoulder
feels suddenly like a holy place, I feel suddenly
like my body is made of marble, not because it's heavy
but because it's shining.

I know she's not asleep because I feel her eyelashes
against my arm when she blinks, like the feet of butterflies
searching for a something bright enough to be mistaken
for a flower. For a moment I forget I'm not alone
in my room and I whisper *I don't know why you like me.*
I can't see her face but feel her smile by my bicep.

You're not afraid to be loud, she says.

There's so much I don't say, I reply.

For now, she says.

Geneva, Geneva, Geneva

With all the other girls asleep
her name is the only song in my ear.

She slips to the floor and guides
my hands to her shoulders. Her skin
feels like warm water
and she squeezes my knuckles, a code,
a request.

I have never given a girl a massage,
I have never sat in a silent silver room
with my hands on the moon's body.

I don't dig into her muscles: mostly
I slide my palms down and across
the slope of her neck,
watching my hands disappear
into shadows, then reappear
again, new.

After a while she tugs me down
then climbs up behind me,
and her hands against my skin
coax my muscles from rock
to sand. Everything sharp
in me, she turns soft.

When her lips connect
with the place where my skin
meets my hair, my blood turns silver,
and I reach up to find her face,
take it in my hands,
and breathe.

CHRISTMAS EVE
On the bus home

it's daylight
but when I close
my eyes against
the sunshine
my eyelids
are still coated
in moondust

I forget for the first time that my hair is red,

pass the mirror in the hall at home
and stop, surprised.

For a moment, the poison
on my head doesn't match
what's in my heart.

I wonder if Medusa

ever found a touch
    soft
        enough

that
all
the
snakes
hissed
themselves
to
sleep.

Texts with Deja

Deja: Your phone was on DnD last night . . .
Alicia: Yeah I was busy
Deja: Busy with . . . ?
Alicia: Nosy!
Deja: I have one! I use it! I smell . . . romance
Alicia: What are you even talking about
Deja: Who's the lucky human
Alicia: I went to Geneva's house for her birthday
Deja: Went on DnD so all your admirers didn't spoil the mood
Alicia: I don't have admirers
Deja: Your phone is always hot. You've got something

Sometimes it's hard to explain

how being the object of someone's desire
isn't the same as being wanted

how always having someone to call
isn't the same as having someone to listen

how someone may stare into your eyes
but sometimes they're looking
at their own reflection

how you can be in a room with a thousand people
and still feel alone.

Winter break is a break because it's broken.

Nothing could make me look forward
to going back to school, but Christmas
in a house of these particular silences
is like riding through a china shop
sitting on a bull's back.

My father stays in Cincinnati,
and my brother stays in his room
and my mother stays in the garage
so I prowl around the house unbothered
on silent, hungry feet,
eating everything in the kitchen

and occasionally cocking my ear
toward the door between me
and my mom, where I expect
to hear her tears, and instead
hear an intermittent laugh.

My brother walks in for snacks,
frowns at my presence. I point
at the garage door:
Has she been dating somebody?
I say it fast before I can take it back.

She's been going to therapy, dumbass,
he says. He takes the whole plate
of Rice Krispie treats Grandma mailed
and disappears again like a ghost
banished back to its grave.

I never go in the garage when my mother's on the phone

But what David says sticks in my head
and before I drift to my room, I reach for the handle
and slowly crack the door.

When I peek out, she looks almost
the way she always looks: wrapped in a coat,
sunk into a folding chair, phone pressed
against her face. There's no smoke
drifting in the air—in fact, I don't smell it
at all. She heard the squeak of the door
and looks my way, and her eyes
are clear, if tired. Just before
I close the door again, her voice
catches my ear, the phone angled away
from her mouth, the words for me:

I see you, Turtle in your shell,
I see you . . . !

I wasn't ready for any of this.
So I pull my head back inside
and lean against the door for a while
before I go to bed.

WEDNESDAY, JANUARY 2
What is a new year

when it's all filled with the same shit?

Alarm.
Toast.
Bus.
Grease stain on khakis.
Fluorescent hallway.
Mrs. Fisher.
The always-open door.
Blake Felipe, her perfect smile.

But then there is Geneva,
waiting by my locker,
Tupperware filled with a pale
something, sprinkled with pistachios—
malai laddu, she says,
her dad's recipe. Her eyes
and it
are sweet, a gift
for the New Year.

Then there's Deja,
hip-bumping me in the hall
between classes, smile
like fresh snow.

Friday! she says.
Dr. Kareem's group!
It's going to be cool.

Her excitement is a virus
I don't mind catching—
I forget to put up my mask
against it.

Dr. Kareem makes us all shy

Even the girls who came into the music room
filled with bubbles and chatter
settle into their chairs like bashful deer
with her chair completing the circle
at the front of the room.

I want to know all your names, she says
and I want to know who you are
what you're afraid of
what your biggest challenge is
what you think you need to overcome
to be the person you want to be.

I can tell by their faces
that most of the other girls
are thinking about college
and scholarships
about being good and kind
and pretty and famous

and I know right away
that agreeing to this group
was a mistake.

Everyone is so optimistic
one foot on a rainbow
ready to ascend.

Everyone wants to impress Dr. Kareem.
Everyone wants to be the best version of themselves.
Everyone wants to shine.

I feel like a stick in the spoke
of a glowing bicycle,
a popcorn kernel that will inevitably
stick in the teeth. I look around
the room and think I am the only
one who brought rain to the parade

which is why I'm surprised when it's
Blake Felipe's turn and rather than speaking
she closes her eyes and cries.

Blake's friends immediately comfort her—

she is the kind of girl who has friends in every room.

I look at the floor—people crying has always made me nervous
especially girls. I'm always afraid that comforting
them will get me too close, that they'll smell
the gay on me, regard my open arms with suspicion.

Blake dries it up quickly, shaking her head.

Sorry, she says. *I'm PMSing. And senior year has been . . . really hard.*

And this is why I know I shouldn't be in this group
because my first reflex isn't to lean in to sisterhood—
instead I feel like curling into myself. How hard

can this year have been, when one is Blake Felipe? To be gold,
to be good, to be guarded by the smiles
of everyone around you?

Let's talk about that, Dr. Kareem says. *What has been really hard for
all of you this year?*

And the circle spins, shy mouths opening one by one, and it feels
a little like Geneva's sleepover, all the grievances slipping out into
    the light.

Blake: college prep
Deja: dealing with racist teachers
Lena Herman: trying to be faster at track so she can get a
    scholarship

They go and go, and eventually it's my turn and I feel the eyes on
    me,
seeing me
taking in the red of me
and I swallow, wishing I could swallow
myself, or the room could. This place
is not for me, I see that now, but
it's too late and they're looking.
Nothing else to lose.

I'm Alicia, I say. *And . . . I guess I've been struggling with . . . feeling
    alone.*

And I don't dare look around the room at first, at the judgment I
    know is waiting.

But when I do finally look up
heads are nodding, including Dr. Kareem's.

Texts with Deja

Deja: It's supposed to be 70 degrees this weekend
Alicia: Thanks, climate change
Deja: Come to my cookout
Alicia: You're having a cookout? In January?
Deja: Carpe diem hoe

The last barbecue I went to was at Sarah's house

and I almost text her to tell her
how when you have so many memories
with one person, it's like a crime scene after they're gone.

Fingerprints everywhere, sometimes visible
and sometimes only popping out at the eye
when a light is shined from a specific angle.

My brother isn't home but Justin is.

Sitting in the kitchen eating a bowl of cereal, chewing
mouth open.

What are you doing here? Where's David?

He says my brother went to pick up his check, and I stare at him
with eyes that I hope are like razors
eyes that demand an answer to the question
I shouldn't have to ask:
Why are you here?

He keeps chewing. For five minutes
the only thing moving
is his mouth, the flash of his teeth
around the silver spoon.

Eventually I go to my room, lock
the door. I stare at my phone
and consider calling my mom
but when it ends up in my hand
pressed against my face
the name I press is DAD.

When he answers he sounds surprised,
like his daughter's name on his screen
is a blast from the past,
a voice from beyond the grave

Is everything okay? he says.

No it is not, I say,
but when he asks me what's going on
I can't speak.

It's like my whole body is a confession
but my throat is a clogged pipe.

I'm so tired of being asked to say
the things that people should
already know.

David is at my door in the morning.

I haven't seen him awake before 8am
in a long time.

I'm fastening my belt, the last piece
of my uniform, and he watches me,
still in flannel sleep pants.

What did you say to Justin?
he says, and my fingers pause.

What? I didn't say anything to him.

He says you were acting weird.
What's your problem?

I stare at his face, remembering
how we used to look alike,
remembering how people used to ask
if we were twins, so little space
between us in their minds.
Everyone saw it: the heaviness
of our brows, the firmness
of our jaws, the wide mouth.
We had an uncle who joked
that we both looked like
a singer named Steven Tyler
because Steven Tyler
looked like both of us, and we
never googled Steven Tyler
because it was better to share
our ignorance and be inside
a joke we didn't understand, together.

Now we both have circles under our eyes
lips pressed tight against our teeth,
eyebrows low.

We have changed beyond recognition
but in the same direction.
We have both mutated
into shadows of who we used to be
and ended up looking the same again,

but I still don't recognize
his face.

Texts with Deja

Deja: you're coming to the cookout today right
Alicia: I think so
Deja: don't chicken out. What, you scared to be around a bunch of
  Black people?
Alicia: no, but I'm scared it's going to rain. Or snow. It's January.
Deja: if it snows we'll just go in my uncle's basement. His house is
  huge.
Alicia: what should I bring?
Deja: just yourself

Deja's uncle's house is huge

Probably the biggest house I've ever seen in person,
the kind of house that looks like a government building
or a historic landmark that no one actually lives in.
The entry floor is marble and the sound of my feet echoes
when I step inside, Deja grinning:

I told you his house was huge. He's a corporate attorney.

I don't really know what that means but I figure
people not knowing what you do is a requirement
for having this much money.

Deja leads me through the museum-house
and it feels so empty and cold until
we get to the backyard, where Deja's family gathers,

spread out across the sprawling grass
like a laughing orchestra.
A wave of *hellos* and *hey honeys*
washes over me like a rush of ocean,
leaving me feeling a little breathless.
Deja's family is huge, a gathering
more like the scope of a family reunion.

You know how to play spades?
someone is asking me, a boy a little older
than us, with eyes that squinch when he smiles.

Leave her alone, Deja says, swats at him
for a moment, but stops when I say yes.

The boy—a cousin: James—squinches
his eyes even more. *Who taught you
to play spades?*

My phone, I say.

That don't count, he laughs, but
he stills gestures for me
to join the table.

James was right.

Playing spades in real life
isn't the same as playing on your phone.

Everyone is yelling at me
and half the people at the table
are standing up halfway through
but everyone is laughing
and I can't remember

the last time
I smiled
this much.

And then I see Deja's uncle.

He's been working the grill, black pants
blending into a black apron, his back to everyone
while he nods to music, flipping burgers.

Meat's done, he shouts, and everyone turns,
abandons card games, James protesting.

I stare at Deja's uncle, tall, built.
His shirt fits a specific way,
like the fabric is as conscious
of his body as women probably are.
I have seen men like this:

men who turn heads, who expect
to curve every neck in the vicinity;
men who gather girls like rose petals
and send them scattering;
men who are so used to hearing yes
that they don't recognize no,
or won't.

I move to the table at the back
of the group, dread pooling
in my stomach like dirty
rain slipped down from the gutter.

He places the meat on the table
and looks up.

Deja points at me before she hands me a plate

Uncle Ronnie, this is my friend Alicia,
and his eyes shift from her face
to mine, noticing me for the first time.

I stare at him, and without meaning to
the Game surfaces in me, like a toxic
cloud rising from the rainwater.
It's like a rubber hammer tapping
a kneecap:
>   reflex
>   instinct
>   automatic

Whenever the part of me that's wounded
unfolds to play the Game, I feel something
in my eyes change: a peeling back,
as raw and red as the meat still uncooked
by the grill. It's a feeling that imitates hunger,
that dares the wolf to look back
and not eat.

Uncle Ronnie straightens, wipes his hands
on his apron, then extends his hand.

How you doing, young lady.
Make sure you get you a burger,
unless you're a vegetarian
or something.

Then he turns his back, cackling,
and returns to the grill.

Deja doesn't notice my face.

She's laughing, yelling at her uncle's back
Not all white girls are vegetarians, Uncle Ronnie!
But he just shrugs, nodding to the music,
adding new burgers to the smoking grill.

Don't listen to him, she says,
and she's pushing the plate into my hands
pointing out which burgers are well done
and which are a little more rare
but the only rare I can think about
is Uncle Ronnie, who has been given teeth
to rip and tear and chooses instead
to smile.

Everyone is eating

and telling jokes, rewinding
to other cookouts, other gatherings,
other games of spades. I listen,
smiling when appropriate,
answering when spoken to,
but my mind is elsewhere.

I'm trying to put my finger
on the thing squirming inside me,
the feeling of embarrassment,
the disappointment and the relief,
all clinging together in a mass
of blushing blood and tissue.

It's not until Uncle Ronnie returns
from the grill with the final plate of burgers,
settling into a seat at the head of the table,
that it hits me. He makes himself a plate
then gazes down the table, his eyes
coming to rest on me and Deja.

So how is school for you girls?
Grades okay?

And then I realize:
he sees me as a child.

It's like a bolt of lightning snaking
down electric from the sky. Almost
every day since I was thirteen,
since my body first began to transform,
I have moved through the world
surrounded by men trying to convince
me and themselves
that there is no such thing as too young
for a woman, or too old for a man,

that there is no such thing
as an unavailable female body.

I have been moving through the world
feeling like a glowing green light,
green for go
      Go
         GO

and Deja's uncle Ronnie is the first person
in a long time to see me,

not the red of my hair,
but me
and decide on his own
to stop.

I feel like a little kid.

I am sixteen years old and have grown
accustomed to feeling
both large and small.

Large, because I take up
so much space in the imaginations
of men, not because
I'm pretty or sexy
or even particularly
interesting, but because
I exist,

and

small, because I am made
to feel that I don't matter at all
and that *no* is a word
I'm not entitled to—
that everything I am
and have done makes me
ineligible for respect.

But in Uncle Ronnie's eyes, I am
neither large nor small,
significant nor insignificant:
I am a sixteen-year-old kid

who does things like
have sleepovers and go to high school
and go to my friend's uncle's
house on weekends.

And he's right, I am, and do,
and even though he's missing
so much about who I am
and what I've done and seen,

the feeling of gratitude
is so heavy and sweet
it feels like sinking into syrup
and drowning in good amber.

Texts with Deja

Alicia: Your family is really cool
Deja: Whoa. You like never text me first! You must have actually had
    fun
Alicia: I did. Thanks for inviting me
Deja: What are friends for?

I wonder if Medusa had friends

if there was anyone who made her want
to fit a hat over her head of snakes

quiet the hissing long enough
to play a game of cards

to drink sweet tea
instead of tears.

But tonight, at home,
I mostly wonder
about Medusa's family—

if her mother was an adder
if her father was an asp
or if they were as she began

flesh

and chose to leave her
to the caves.

Sometimes I can't look at my hands

because if I stare at them for too long I start to realize
they're attached to my body
and that my body is real.

I've heard people call it a spiral—
the mental cave I fall down when remembering:

all the girls I was before

all the parts of myself I've lost

all the people I could have been.

Sometimes when I look at my hands
it's like seeing a face in an airport
that belongs to someone
you thought was already dead.

Geneva has started waiting at my locker

and it's almost like on Valentine's Day when you get to school
wondering if there will be a red heart waiting at your desk,
a rose, a massive stuffed bear.

Geneva is more than all these things, and less obvious—
her smile is like a secret just for me, even though
now that we have started walking down the hall
shoulder to shoulder, people sometimes turn
and look, wondering.

I can't tell if they're worried for her safety—
new girl unaware whose proximity she's entered—
or if they see the thing that I feel:

a sun rising out of the teacup of her smile,
filling the space between us with light,
warming me for the few minutes
before we part again for class.

So when there's a note on my locker

I stubbornly think *Geneva,*
even as my stomach sinks.

She doesn't have my phone number
and although she gave me hers
I haven't had the guts to text her yet.

It is Geneva.

Geneva
Geneva
Geneva

But the piece of paper poking through
the vent is white and lined, and it slips
out into my fingers when I tug.

Then I see blue ink,
and everything I have been trying
not to see, trying not to know

is here.

Seven words, written
in neat looping print:

I know about the Colonel.
Me too.

Nothing can be undone.

Not coming to this school.
Not running track.
Not walking into the Colonel's class
    that day, and
    the other days.
Not sealing my mouth like a tomb,
    silent.
Not having sex.
Not telling Sarah about it.
Not lying to my parents
    every single day.

Not reading this note.

Jacob Wheeler catches me at the bus stop again

and when I turn away, start to jog,
this time he sprints, his gazelle legs
closing the distance before I even know
it's a race. His hands are out
in front of me like he's trying to flag
down a runaway train, like he sees
the red of me and is offering water
to calm the flames.

Just wait, just wait, he says.
Please. For a second.
I know you don't want
to run, but Tabitha Watts rolled
her ankle and we need someone
for the 4x4 tomorrow.
Please. Just one day.
Just one race. A scrimmage.
I won't bother you again
but we need your help for
just
one
race.

Coach Tinsley is watching from the school door

and his posture is like Jacob Wheeler's, poised
as if on eggshells. Not like they think I am glass
and might crack, but that I am a bomb
that might explode. Their nervousness
makes me want to scream, the idea

that *I* am the thing everyone is afraid of
when they walk the halls with a wolf.

The bus is coming, and he sees it,
and he knows it's my escape pod,
and he says one more time: *Please.*

I'm getting on the bus.
Tomorrow, he shouts after me,
tomorrow at four!

The doors close behind me,
and the feeling that overwhelms
my body is like thirst.

I sit by the window, head on glass,
try to think of beautiful
peaceful things:

Lilacs, petals on a river,
Geneva, paint on her fingertips.

I stare out at the passing blur
of traffic until I'm swallowed.

I keep imagining the Colonel's closed door

and it transforms into a bone
caught in my throat.

I can't swallow.
I can't speak.

All I can think about
is that I
knew.

Whenever I close my eyes
I see the always-open door, closed.

And I knew what it meant
and never raised a fist to knock.

Never summoned my courage,
never let my rage turn me into a weapon.

I just walked past the door quietly,
the lamb I always say I'm not.

I ask Stephanie to put me on back line

and she's confused at first, because I haven't made sandwiches
since I was first hired, haven't sliced beef for a year.

There must be something in my eyes, on my face
like a tattoo or a stain

because she agrees, moves Debbie up to the drive-thru
and I tuck myself into the shadow of the microwaves
and refrigerators, assembling sandwiches and salads
with robotic precision. It feels good not to speak.

It feels good not to engage.
It feels good to be a pair of hands.
It feels good to be good for one thing.

Eventually, though, we run out of beef,
and I plod to the back, remove one of the steaming
meteors of meat from the oven,
plop it onto the slicer.

I watch the mass become thin layers,
think of Debbie's finger separating

from her hand, all those years ago
but in this very spot.

How many fingers have been lost
and never found, how many girls
like me have been shoved through
the slicer, mangled, coming out
unrecognizable on the other side?

How many of us walk past each other
every day, not knowing what we've lost,
not knowing we are missing
the same pieces?

Texts with Deja

Alicia: has anything bad ever happened to you?

Deja: of course

Alicia: do you want to tell me?

Deja: I mean, I could. Some of it is hard to say?

Alicia: that bad?

Deja: yes and no. sometimes it's just not big stuff. A million little
things. Sand on a beach.

Alicia: At school?

Deja: Yes. But this whole world wants me to be smaller than I am.
Smaller and neater.

Alicia: like it's putting you through a slicer

Deja: it's more like the sand. You know sea glass? The sand and the
salt wearing it down smaller and smoother every day, year after
year. And I'm not even allowed to be mad about it

Alicia: Everyone hates angry girls

Deja: yeah but I'm talking about being Black. I don't know if you've
noticed, but when we're in ISAP it's bc I said "please don't be

racist" & you said "fuck you Mrs. Fisher you look like a sardine
  somebody slapped"

Alicia: lmfao I've never said that

Deja: but you see my point.

Alicia: Taken. They'd make me captain of debate team if I said what
  you say

Deja: I really am going to quit that shit

Alicia: like actually?

Deja: no lol fuck Clay Bevin

Alicia: For the record, I like you big and bright

Deja: Yeah? what about sharp?

Alicia: especially that

Something I've learned from Deja

Bodies
    are classified
    as dangerous
            for different reasons
            depending
on who they belong to.

We have a calendar at home that's always empty

but when I get home I see my mother has written something
in red for Friday next week, the same day as Dr. Kareem's group:
eye exam for Alicia.

We have to do this every year if I want to avoid
the glasses I gave up to run track.

I guess contacts aren't necessary since I don't run
anymore, but the thought draws my eye

to the calendar's square of tomorrow, white
and empty. I remember Jacob Wheeler's face,

the appeal between his eyebrows: *please*.
I'm out of shape. They must know.

The part of me that is a primal beast,
shrinking from fire, wonders if this is a trick,

a ruse to draw me into the light, only
to bring a club down on my skull.

The idea makes me bristle, a bear
lumbering down through my veins.

I would never call the track mine, but
when I ran, the wind itself felt

like it belonged to me—*Pry it
from my cold dead hands,* I think,

but then I think, *Well,
someone kind of already did.*

First text conversation with Geneva

Alicia: Hi. This is Alicia.
Geneva: At long last! What are you doing?
Alicia: Lying on my bed.
Geneva: In your Meat Palace uniform
Alicia: What is it with you and my uniform
Geneva: Just teasing. How was work?
Alicia: I have all my fingers.
Geneva: Three cheers for no blood. How many burgers did you
make?

Alicia: You know that Meat Palace doesn't serve burgers right

Geneva: They don't?

Alicia: lol no

Geneva: Oh.

Texts with Geneva: Part 2

Geneva: Has your hair always been red?

Alicia: No.

Geneva: Send me a pic from before

Alicia: Why

Geneva: Because.

Alicia: [image]

Geneva: A bathing suit pic!

Alicia: It's the only one I have on my phone with my natural hair

Geneva: Are you trying to seduce me?

Alicia: Would it be working?

Geneva: Yes. But that would be true no matter what picture you sent

Texts with Geneva: Part 3

Alicia: What are you doing

Geneva: Sitting on the couch with my mom

Alicia: Just sitting?

Geneva: Watching Netflix. She likes crime shows. We're solving murders

Alicia: 10pm on a school night. Tsk tsk

Geneva: I'll sleep on the bus.

Alicia: What are you doing tomorrow afternoon

Geneva: Nothing. Why . . . ?

Alicia: If I asked you to come with me to something, would you?

Geneva: Yes

Alicia: I thought you would say "it depends on the something"

Geneva: It doesn't

Texts with Geneva: Part 4

Alicia: Tell me a story about you

Geneva: Once upon a time there was a girl who lived in a cold
kingdom in the north. She knew its ten thousand lakes by heart,
and one time she did yoga on the rocks for three hours until the
sun set and she should've gotten lost because it was so dark
but she knew the path so well she was fine. She found her way
through the trees and the lake kept her company. It looked like
there were ten thousand moons on its surface. She tried to paint
it when she got home but nothing could do it justice so she
always pictures it just before she goes to sleep instead. It was
the night she found her way.

Alicia: did she live happily ever after?

Geneva: we'll see

Thinking about princesses and peas

In the story, the queen tests the girl at the gates
with a tower of mattresses, a pea at the base.
Only a princess would feel it, and the girl does.

I'm riding the city bus to school in the morning,
thinking about Geneva, about how her singular
presence in my life makes the rocking ocean
seem somehow more still.

And I am not this princess, because in the story
the girl was destined to marry the son
of the queen and the concept of anyone's son
has lost all appeal. But
I do think that if I were to take all the weights

from my shoulders and lay them down
to sleep on, with Geneva at the bottom,
I would still feel her.

I would still feel her.

I forgot about Dr. Kareem's girl group

until her assistant came around to the classrooms,
gathering us all up, herding us down the hall
toward the music room. We have to pass my locker
and I glance in its direction, wondering
if there will be another note, a white banner
flagging me down. There is nothing.

Correction: there is nothing *today*.
There will always be something.
I have already read the note—
me too burned onto the backs
of my eyelids: there is no
unseeing what has already
been staring at me
out of the deep,
unknowable dark.

Dr. Kareem asks us how our weekends were

and people offer their college application answers. Everyone
is still hell-bent on impressing her, looking for ways
to draw her honey-brown eyes to their face, their story.

Deja, though, offers something that turns our heads:
I got into a fight with my aunt, she says. *She was talking
about R. Kelly and how all those girls he raped
knew what they were getting into. She didn't even care
that most of them were my age.* I know Deja
well enough now to hear the tremble in her voice.
I wonder if the aunt was one of the smiling women
I met in Uncle Ronnie's vast backyard.

*It's not always men who are on the wrong side
of things,* Dr. Kareem said. *Sometimes we are our own
worst enemy, fighting battles with people
hurt by the weapons formed against us both.*

What do you mean weapons? says Prya, sounding
unconvinced, suspicious.

*Any time you feel that your personhood
has been turned into a liability,
a target on your back,
a trip wire at your feet,
someone has put a weapon to your throat.*

Dr. Kareem sounds so sure when she says this,
so unapologetic for what I know would make
boys laugh or roll their eyes, what would make
some fathers sigh at our drama,

that we all sit quiet, and then one by one
our hands start to rise.

Weapons formed against us

Annlia: *Our periods. There's like a whole industry of companies
and products that exist to make us feel bad about periods.*

Lena: *Hormones. Like when they say trans girls can't run track
and compete against other girls. It's so stupid because I have
friends who are cis girls and they're faster than a lot of cis boys.
If I'm faster, then I'm just faster. It's like they're insulting both
of us.*

Eugenia: *Family. My brothers never have to do dishes or help with
dinner, but I always have to. But we all have to do homework.
So they have all this free time that I just . . . never have. All these
empty hours that I don't get. It adds up.*

Deja: *Our hair. If it's short, you're a lesbian. If it's long, you think
you're cute. And there's different rules for Black girls. White girls
can wear cornrows and dye their hair all kinds of colors but it's
like it means something different on my head.*

Tierra: *Why do white teachers always act like Black girls are more
mature? Ever since I was in first grade they've been treating me
like an adult.*

Alicia: *I'm so tired of being called a slut.*

The room had already been quiet

because something about Deja and Tierra
saying the word *white* multiple times
in a row has the effect of a Taser.

But now everyone shifts and stares,
because with the exception
of Deja, all of them have probably
called me a slut
a hoe
a whore
a skank
at least once
even just in passing,

and hearing the slut
address her own rumor
is like the beef at Meat Palace
sitting up on the bun
and discussing what it's like
to be a sandwich.

The sandwich
is not supposed
to talk

The meat
is supposed
to stay meat

and everyone is shifting
in their seats, including me,
and I have so many things
I could say, and it all feels
so close to my teeth,

but all the words disappear
down my throat

and I'm just
a sandwich again.

Dr. Kareem has the look of someone drilling for oil,

like a fine black mist has just appeared on her fingertips.
She gazes at us, drinking in our silence,
and I'm grateful at least that she doesn't stare
only at me. When she finally speaks
she says

Let me tell you a list
of things that don't exist:

Flying pigs
Dinosaurs—at least not anymore
Zombies
The Queen of Canada
Freddy Krueger
and
Sluts

Everything Dr. Kareem says feels like quartz

Hard and flat, no room for argument to seep in,
flawless. She lets her eyes wander the room, searching
for someone brave enough to argue, and though Blake
Felipe narrows her eyes, everyone listens

and so Dr. Kareem goes on.

The invention of the slut
is the same kind of lie
that called Medusa a monster.

Depending on the story,
Medusa was a whore
who seduced men toward destruction,

or maybe she was just a beautiful
girl in a world in which
beauty is power.

In most tellings
she was raped by a god
then transformed
into a monster.

Whatever the reason,
our history focuses
on her monstrousness:
the way she would turn men
into stone with one gaze,
her scream like a sword.

So much of who we are told
to be
is a suit sewn with myths:

Virginity? A violent scam.
The hymen never existed
to measure purity or chastity—
one more invention
designed to bind us.

Even the concept of ugly
is a farce, the hatechild
of patriarchy and white supremacy.

The history you are taught
the future you are instructed to imagine—
spokes in the same crushing wheel.

Some women find escape
in domination—your teachers
who wear whiteness like a badge.

I have to ask you, girls:
how many of you have walked
through this world as a woman,
placed into a box that's too tight,

and how many of you have ever
    for a moment
wished you had a nest
of snakes upon your head
to do all the things
you can't yourself?

We're all silent when we leave the music room

and we all have different destinations
but as we spread down the halls
it feels a little like something
from the room is following us,
that even after we've left
Dr. Kareem's words cling
to us like slime

or maybe
like pollen.

I finally google Medusa

because since the library with Deja
it's like the woman and her snakes
have haunted my steps.

The photos online are different
from the book: so many
interpretations of her face
and her life
but it's generally agreed upon:

Medusa was beautiful and the god
Poseidon noticed. He followed her
into Athena's temple and
"had sex with her."
Athena was angry and turned
Medusa into a monster with a terrible
face and snakes for hair, and at first I thought
this was revenge, so that Medusa
could kill at will, but then I read
that it was punishment.

For Medusa.

But that is the part
that history kind of skips. The part
that all the stories tell instead
is the part that came after:

Perseus, the hero, comes to slay
the beast that is the snake-haired woman
and when he finally took her head
everyone rejoiced, including Athena.

One thing I notice is that no one
really talks about Poseidon at all
and as I sit in Mrs. Fisher's class reading
from my phone, I think
That figures.

Are you there, Medusa? It's me, Alicia.

Of all the things you turned to stone
with the killing eyes you didn't ask for,
I wonder how many times
you tried looking in the mirror,

wondering if now that you had transformed
from girl to monster

it was possible
to transform again
this time into a rock
that
    feels
    sees
    remembers
        nothing.

Letter to Medusa: Part 2

Not only did gods and goddesses alike
join forces in your destruction,
they gave the man with the sword
extraordinary tools to turn you into dust:

Athena gave Perseus a special shield,
Hermes gave winged sandals,
Hephaestus gave a sword,
and Hades gave his very own cloak of invisibility.

It seems odd to me that you
were just one girl,
and mortal,
but you scared the gods and goddesses
enough
to send all those weapons
in the effort of closing
your eyes.

Mrs. Fisher sends me to ISAP for using my phone

and I should have known it was coming,
because whenever I am actually in her classroom
it's like my presence is a pebble in her shoe,
a hair in her soup. Her eyes actually light up
when she glimpses my phone under the desk,
she's borderline gleeful when she grabs the walkie-talkie.

If my life is a tragedy, and I don't know
if it is, then maybe Mrs. Fisher is Athena
or Hera, one of the women who cut Medusa down
without ever having to carry a sword.

Mr. Upton, the security guard, comes for me,
escorts me out, and when I pass Mrs. Fisher
I look her straight in the face
and even though every day on this earth
still makes me want to cry
I still feel a stab of satisfaction
from the way she refuses
to meet
my eyes.

Halfway to ISAP, Mr. Upton stops at the water fountain

just as Tierra Pryor comes around the corner
carrying a hall pass.

It's been three hours since
Dr. Kareem's girl group
and I wonder if Tierra
has been thinking about Medusa
as much as I have.

It's hard to tell, but she does pause,
glances at Mr. Upton,
and then whispers
Please
don't forget
about the scrimmage.

She thinks she's persuading me
to jump out of a plane.
She doesn't know

264

that my track shoes
have been in my locker
for months
waiting for me to
remember how to fly.

Texts with Geneva in ISAP

Geneva: So have you decided if you're going to do "the thing" you
   told me about?

Alicia: Not yet

Geneva: Are you going to tell me what "the thing" is?

Alicia: ●●●

Geneva: Are you getting an abortion or something?

Alicia: What? No.

Geneva: Why else would you be so secretive?

Alicia: lol It's a track meet, Jesus

Geneva: You run track?

Alicia: I used to

Geneva: "Today" and "used to" seem like opposite things

Alicia: I'm deciding if I want to again

Geneva: What's stopping you

Alicia: I'm not sure

When Mr. West takes the ISAP kids to the bathroom

I sit down to pee and stare at my thighs
in the weird fluorescent school light.
They are the pale yellow of my winter skin,
starting to sprout hairs from where I shaved

last week. My legs haven't seen the sun
since the Day, the Time, the Incident.

I haven't worn shorts since the Colonel's
fingertips made them impossible. Blue
and white, our school colors, in a crumpled
ball on my locker floor. I can't wear those.

Touching the shoes will be hard enough,
tying myself into those laces, walking
in my own footsteps. Am I actually
going to do this? Am I actually
going to attempt to be
who I used to be?

Does that person still exist?
Has she been waiting
for me?

Texts with Deja

Deja: Tierra says you're thinking about running today?
Alicia: I didn't say that
Deja: But are you?
Alicia:
Deja: But are you?
Deja: Hello?

It's one long, straight line

from ISAP to my locker, and I make my way
wondering if the shoes will still fit,

or if everything about me that feels as if
it has both swollen and shrunk
is true. I am overcome with memories

the way my legs used to shake as I approached
the line, the way my lungs would feel small
as I bent, fingertips to pavement.
     And then the shot.

And my legs would find their courage
and my lungs would open to the air
and together me and this body
would fly, my hair streaming
like gold snakes behind me.

I have no idea what my face
looked like when I ran.
I never cared.

I'm not even
at the track yet and my legs
have already begun to tremble,
and I walk slowly because of this,
staring down. So it's not until
I have almost reached my locker
that I see it:

the note.

A white triangle like the fin
of a shark protruding
into the hallway's swift current.

It takes me a long time to reach it—
I am walking along the bottom

of the ocean: the weight of the sea
pulling me back and down.

When it's in my fingers I wonder
if I have the strength not to read it,
but it inevitably opens in my hand,
the blue loops swimming together
and crushing into my eyes:

I think I'm going to tell.
Will you?

Texts from Deja

Deja: I'm going to come to the meet
Deja: I'll be cheering you on!
Deja: You nervous? I can give you a pep talk!

Texts from Geneva

Geneva: I'm by your locker—where are you?
Geneva: Want me to meet you at the track?
Geneva: Are you okay?

Texts from a random

Him: I just passed your Meat Palace 😊 Do you work today?
Alicia: No but I'm free
Him: Oh nice. Where can I pick you up?
Alicia: Anywhere

I'm running

I might as well
be barefoot
the way
every step
hurts
the way
each time
my feet
hit the earth
I feel
my bones
rattle.

Don't bother
with bus stops
or sidewalks,

the only aim
is to stay
in shadow
is to stay
in secret
is to stay
burning so hot
that the smoke
obscures
the flames.

His car smells like cedar

the little green tree hanging from the rearview
swinging in pointless circles.

He reminds me of a cop, the smile
that is part uniform, part disguise.

I've ridden alongside enough wolves
to know that he likes this part,
the part where he gets to believe
he is convincing me of something:

the part where he imagines a wall
that he approaches with a pickaxe,
an iron gate that he steals up to
with a fistful of keys, trying each
one while grinning full-fang.

He likes imagining that I am a peach
he is coaxing into a pie.

He imagines he is a mouthful
of teeth, and he is.

What he doesn't account for
is the fact that the peach
is searching for the knife,
for the bite,

the peach is proving a point
even if it means the uprooting
of her core.

Nothing is simple

His name is Deon and he doesn't know
how old I am because he never asks

even though I'm wearing a
school uniform

even though I have hanging cuticles

even though I have scuffed shoes

even though I don't have a haircut,
just hair.

I catch glimpses of myself
in the window, all the things
that make me feel like a child
all the things that Deja's
uncle Ronnie saw that painted
a red X through my viability,
and wonder if it's a matter
of vision—

those that see
and those that don't—

or a matter of perspective:

those that see and know,
and those that see
and choose not to care.

His house is clean.

I have seen the dens of wolves
and they all look different:

waxed floors
laundry on the banister
pots on the stove
no pots at all

the only thing
that's always the same
is the wolf
who lives there.

I am here but I am
nowhere.

I think of Medusa
stone
I think of Geneva
  soft

I think of all in between,
all the betweens I am.

Texts from Geneva that I see later

Geneva: You weren't at work after school.

Geneva: I got some mozzarella sticks and waited for you. I see why
people eat fast food. Kind of.

Geneva: Something made you disappear today. I wish I knew what.
I'm here if you want to talk.

Text from Geneva at midnight

Geneva: Your friend Deja was worried about you. You have a lot of
people that love you, just so you know. Whatever you're dealing
with, you don't have to deal with it alone.

Instead of telling my story, I ask her to tell me another story about her

Geneva: Once upon a time there was a girl who loved her father
and this didn't mean she didn't love her mother but to her
father she was like a jewel in his crown and he never minded
when she was under his feet while he made chicken korma,
and sometimes he would boop her nose and leave an orange
dot of turmeric. The girl remembers that even now. The girl's
father had no family in the cold land of the north, the land of her
mother, and losing her father made everything colder still. In this
new place the girl has aunties who make korma for her because
her mother wouldn't know where to begin and sometimes the
aunties still make comments about how the girl's father should
have married a woman from Pakistan and sometimes the girl
agrees which makes her feel guilty even though she loves her
mother. The girl likes it here better even though her mother is
lonely for the lakes so sometimes the girl still tries to paint them.
Their house is full of lakes but empty of her father.

Alicia: What was his name?

Geneva: Arjan

Alicia: Does the girl paint portraits of him?

Geneva: No.

Alicia: Why not?

Geneva: Sometimes it feels like painting is magic, and the girl
dreams that painting him would bring him back. She knows that

when she paints him and he's still gone, it will feel like losing him
for good.
Alicia: Maybe when you bring back something you've lost, it returns
in a different form
Geneva: Maybe

Thank god it's Saturday

I don't think I could take walking into school
and seeing Deja
Tierra
Jacob Wheeler
Coach Tinsley,
watching their faces decide
whether or not I am worth
speaking to, my absence
worth interpretation.

In my state of isolation,
in the cave whose dark
I have grown so accustomed to,
I am unused to disappointing
anyone but myself.

I'm getting my khakis out of the dryer

when my mother appears at the top of the basement
steps. I know it's her and not my brother
by the soft cough that passes her lips
whenever she is about to start a fight.

You don't need the pants, she says.
You're not going to work.

Yes I am, I call up.
I go in at 10.

I called and told them
you weren't coming in, she says,

and I think I've misheard her
until I turn and look up
the mountain of stairs,
at her face staring down,
at her arms crossed not
over her chest in defiance
but over her stomach
as if in pain. *Is someone*
dead? I say. I'm always asking
if someone is dead, looking
for a shadow bleaker
than my own, but all she does
is disappear.

She's waiting for me in the kitchen

I saw someone drop you off last night.
Your brother told me you've been going out
at night, and last night

I waited and watched, and I couldn't see
who it was but I can tell you it wasn't a boy,

it wasn't a girl, it wasn't someone your age,
it wasn't someone who should be

dropping you off after dark, it wasn't
Sarah, it wasn't her mom or brother,

it wasn't someone I know, it wasn't
someone whose car you should be in

and all I want to know, Alicia, is what
is making you so afraid of life

that you are putting yourself
in the way of something so sure
to crush you?

I should feel so many things

but in this moment all I want to do
is go to my brother's door,
knock on it politely,
and when he answers,
throw my fist against
his face.

But he's not home.

Of course.

The men
in my family
enjoy ripping
open the cushions
and when feathers
begin to fly,
crashing on another couch.

Texts with David

Alicia: I can't believe you snitched, you fucking bastard. I can't believe after months of not saying shit to me you run tell Mom instead of talking to me

David: You seem to be operating under the illusion that talking to you has been an option for the last eight months

Alicia: Oh, now it's my fault? What, because I'm *so rude* to your little friend? Fuck him and you

David: You make everyone nervous

Alicia: ME? ME.

David: Me and Mom are worried about you

Alicia: Worry about yourself, cunt

Thinking about notes

The papers that were slipped into my locker
are nesting under my pillow, not at risk
of giving me bad dreams since
I rarely sleep. It's daylight

but I lie staring at my ceiling
thinking about the notes
I used to scribble to my brother,
tucked under his door
like evening prayers.

I can't remember
what any of them
ever said, what David
and I spent so much
time and ink relaying
to each other.

I know I kept at least one,
squirreled into the shoe box
under my desk. I retrieve
it, find his handwriting
easily, always so mechanical
and square:

DEAR ALICIA

I HOPE YOU HAVE A GOOD DAY
AT SCHOOL AND MS. RUPE
ISN'T MEAN TO YOU. SHE
WAS MEAN TO ME, BUT MAYBE
YOUR FIFTH GRADE
WILL BE DIFFERENT THAN MY
FIFTH GRADE, MAYBE SHE
WON'T KNOW YOU
ARE MY SISTER AND SHE WILL
GIVE YOU A BREAK. REMEMBER
YOU CAN ALWAYS GO
TO MS. HARRIS'S CLASS
DURING LUNCH. SHE ALWAYS
LET SENSITIVE KIDS
HANG OUT THERE WHEN
WE NEEDED TO.

I stare at the words
sensitive kids and *we*
and think my brother must have
at some point imagined
himself as a rabbit,

and I wonder what
animal he is now.

Texts with Geneva

Alicia: I didn't say it last night so I'll say it now. Sorry I ghosted
Geneva: Are you still feeling like a ghost?
Alicia: Yes
Geneva: If it helps . . . I can still see you.

What I don't text Geneva

What if I'm feeling
more monster
than ghost

what if my hair
turns to cobras

what if my eyes
turn to machine guns

what if my tongue
is forked and bloody

will you still see me?
will you still see me?

Texts with Deja

Alicia: Remember what I said in Dr. Kareem's group?
Deja: Yes.
Alicia: I keep thinking about what you said about a circle, or a heart,

or a box, how the farther somebody gets from the middle—
from what everyone demands they be—the happier they are.
The freer they are. I'm not saying you're wrong, but I don't feel
happy. Or free.

Deja: Never?

Alicia: Sometimes.

Deja: Do you want to talk about it?

Alicia:

Deja: I guess I should have expected that.

Alicia: I'm sorry. I'm not a very good friend.

Deja: Why not?

Alicia: I don't know how.

Deja: Better get some training wheels, doll

My mother waits in the kitchen all day

When I come out at 2pm she is eating a cheese sandwich
and drinking chocolate milk. She stares at me,
then down at her plate.

Dairy when I'm sad, she says.
Some things never change.
Do you have things like that?

At first I don't think I'll speak,
but the words come on their own,
the quiet house, the empty
doors, the silent garage,
all like a cup I have to fill:

Chocolate when I'm sad, I say.
Cheese when I'm angry.
Salt when I'm scared.

Grab yourself some food then, she says.
Let's talk.

I go to the fridge and stand
in its white glare. All the shelves
are full, but I don't know what
to reach for.

I'm supposed to be talking

I'm supposed to be pouring out my heart.
My mother is looking at me
for the first time in months,
actually seeing me and not the apparitions
of her marriage
her mother
her past and future,
and still my throat
is the clogged pipe,
stopped up with debris,
with garbage and mess.

I think my crying might make her
feel better, to know that something
in her daughter is still breathing
is still bloody and alive.

But maybe nothing is
because I end up eating
peanut butter and jelly,
which is what I eat
when I'm feeling lonely.

Thoughts about silence

When Sarah and I were in sixth grade, she didn't speak
to her parents for nine days, a silent strike
in protest of their decision to keep her home
from the church camping trip.

Her silence was a demand, her silence
still contained words. I don't know
what my silence is saying.

My mother and I sit on the couch
watching a movie from the 2000s
and everyone is carrying
huge purses and tiny dogs
and I barely catch a word of it
because I am trying so hard to listen
to the inside of my head
searching for the thing that is binding
my tongue. My mother probably thinks
I'm depressed. She thinks
whatever cloud has stretched over my life
is one that she saw in the Parenting Teenagers
Handbook. She is always
blaming things on herself, she probably
thinks this is a symptom of divorce
has probably been researching
family therapy, self-help books.

She is so good. It doesn't occur to her
that all the clouds in this storm
stirred because of me, and opening
my mouth will only add hail
to the rain and thunder.

I watch her watching the movie
and imagine my silence as a bunker.
But when I really think about it
I don't know who it's protecting:
her
or me
or Him.

"You can tell me"

She says it midway through another movie.
We've been on the couch all day.
Maybe she thinks she can wait me out.
She doesn't know I've been holding
everything in for so long already.

Even if you don't tell me everything, she says.
Even if you just want to say a piece.

I'm not friends with Sarah anymore
I say, before she can ask more questions,
before her tongue in her mouth becomes
a sword in my heart. *She stopped talking
to me in April. She said she never
wants to see me again.*

Beside me my mother takes a deep
breath. She's going to ask why,
she's going to do the thing
that mothers do, when they
can't help but transform
into scissors, needle, scalpel:
surgeons over the lives
of their children.

Sarah was always a judgy
little bitch, my mother says,

and I almost snap my neck
turning to see her face,
and when I see her raised
eyebrows, her half smile,
I can't help but laugh,
a sound that rises and rolls
out of me like magma,
so fast and hot
I can't stop.

I'm still laughing when she says
You've probably been feeling
really lonely, and I realize then
the faint, faint line that exists
between laughter and tears.

It's been a long time since I fell asleep

with my mother's fingers in my hair.

On the border between awake
and asleep, I can imagine
I'm a baby again,
young and new and without scars.

Part of me thinks I'm dreaming
when I hear my mother's voice
trickle through, but I'm not:

I read that anger can grow
of trauma. That it can turn
a human into a volcano.

I want you to know I'm here.
It's okay to be angry.
I can stand your lava.

I'm glad my eyes are closed.
Open, I might cry,
and I'm not ready
for anything
that doesn't
burn.

I'm still asleep on the couch when David comes home

the smell of weed and cats surging in alongside him,
Justin at his heels. Justin goes on to David's room

but through my half-closed eyes, David pauses
by the couch and looks down at me
for a long moment

before he lets out a breath in the low light.
His steps down the hall are heavy and slow
and I don't know if he's drunk or sad,
or something else I cannot name.

TUESDAY, JANUARY 22
Short week for MLK

and no one is taking anything seriously except Mrs. Fisher,
who sends me to ISAP for not wearing a belt.
Cussing her out gets old—when I leave I just say
Thanks for the stellar education, Margaret,
and people laugh, but I don't care.

Mr. West waves me in wearily, and it's just us
two in the silent gray room, the voices
of the Temptations like a warm gold light
in the corner. Sitting staring at the wall
I gradually realize that I'm not nervous.

I am alone in a room with a man, Mr. West,
and no follicle of my hair, no cell of my blood
ripples with anxiety. I glance at him
every few minutes, the way his face folds
down to study the book in his hands.
He's reading something called *Salvage
the Bones,* and I wonder who
taught him not to howl
at the moon.

The door opens and I already know, somehow,
it will be Deja. Mr. Upton leads her in.

What are we protesting today? Mr. West says,
not looking up from his book.

Everything, Mr. West, she says.
Everything.
I hear that, lil sister. Take a seat.

She knew I was there.

She walks straight toward me, and students in ISAP
are supposed to sit two desks apart, but today
she comes and places a hand on the chair
right next to me, glances back at Mr. West.

He looks up, feeling our proximity,
and the brown eyes behind his glasses
take us in, take in whatever prayer
is on our faces. One hand rises, waves
us off. Deja sits down.

Do you want to talk, she whispers.
      Not really.

You have to talk to me sometime. You have
to tell me what's up with you.
      Do I?

Did something happen? Something I don't see?
I can only sigh.

Dear Athena,

Some people on the internet say
that what you did to Medusa
was a gift, so she could take revenge

on men like Poseidon
      (who *wasn't* just a man)
for doing things like what Poseidon
      did.

But I call bullshit, Athena.
I don't know who you paid
to sell that version of yourself

but if you gave a shit
about Medusa

then why did you give Perseus
the goddamn shield
he would use to kill her?

You were a goddess
and Poseidon a god
so if you wanted revenge
why didn't you
take it?

Jacob Wheeler and Tierra Pryor are dressed

for practice. I pass them in the hallway and feel
my body tense as their eyes pass over me,
    seeing
and then consciously
      unseeing.

Last week they could see me,
but then I ghosted.

Maybe some ghosts
haunt
themselves.

The Sixth Sense

I watched it with my mom once when I was thirteen
and she was so excited about the twist, couldn't wait
to see if I caught it. I didn't, but I was less interested

in the ghost of Bruce Willis than I was in the little boy
who saw blood everywhere he turned, little girl
ghosts vomiting their secrets into his bed
when all he wanted to do was be normal.

I don't want to be that ghost for Geneva—
she has her own problems, her own aching
heart. So when she meets me at my locker
after school, I want to truly disappear,
want to watch my skin turn into nothing.

But then she smiles
and every cell of me is visible.

Geneva walks me to work

It's hard to avoid the eyes of someone like her
who sees so much, seemingly without looking.
We've walked three blocks when she takes my hand
and it's like the moment before a tornado
touches ground, when all the world goes still
and silent. Or maybe it's the moment after
the storm has passed, or maybe the moment
right in the center, the eye, when
the storm blinks, and you think you're safe.

My grandma used to tell us all
that when a tornado was on the horizon,
to open every window of the house—
to let the storm air in so that the pressure
didn't burst every pane into a roar
of glass. I know this was not good
advice, but with Geneva's hand in mine

I walk down the street toward Meat Palace
with the urge to throw open
every window of myself
let in the heady scent of storm

because in the middle of all this
it feels as if I'm going to burst either way
and maybe I would rather smell
the rain and look the storm
right in the eye.

I'm not good at being honest

even though Geneva makes me want to be

so when she asks me to tell her
a story about myself this time

my brain is a minefield
of all the things I can't quite
look at, let alone say.
She thinks I'm so brave
so tough—
she doesn't know
that a white piece of paper
with blue ink sends me spiraling
scattering into pieces.

But she asks again,

and the only thing I can say
is that when I hold her hand
I remember being small
and walking through the market
touching the smooth skins
of apples and apricots—

how I always loved art
class, the still life,
capturing light.

I say

You should paint your father

and she says

Maybe I'll paint you

and I say

Or you could paint your father

and her smile is as soft
and sweet
as a plum.

Geneva asks to come in and sit in the lobby

but I see Terry's car in the parking lot, and I know
he would be an asshole, tell her she had to buy
a sandwich per hour or some bullshit. So we say

goodbye, and I let her hand go, and everything
about watching her walk back the way we came
is like watching a unicorn retreat

into a storybook. But that makes it sound
like Geneva is magic, and she isn't.
She is an ordinary girl who is not
ordinary at all.

Because Terry is on the clock I have to take out my nose ring

and I can't ask to work back line because it's only
Rodney, me, and Debbie, and Rodney doesn't do register.
So me and Debbie take drive-thru and Terry

handles the counter, which is the easiest place
to work this time of day, but Debbie is a good
partner and we roll through the orders:

please and *thank you* and *have a nice day*
here's some extra napkins
what kind of sauce would you like
here's your change

It's easy to take my mind off all the things
that eat my wooden brain like termites.
Thanks for choosing Meat Palace, what can
I get for you today? Over and over
and they answer, sometimes rude
and sometimes not, always hungry,
and everything is fine
until the voice that answers
belongs to Sarah.

She orders a beef and cheddar with no sauce

which is what she always ordered when she would come hang
out while waiting for me to get off work she sounds close
to the order speaker, which means she's probably driving,
which means she has her permit, which also means
her father is in the car, or worse, her mother,
or maybe her brother Reese who once
told me he was praying the gay kid
in his class would go to hell even
though that kid, Sam, still went
to church three times a week

my heart feels like it's been
dropped in the deep fryer
scalded to nothing and
by the time Sarah's
car pulls around
and I see her
face smiling
I just want
to turn
into
ash.

Debbie takes the money from Sarah's hand

I almost warn her, *Debbie watch out, she bites*
but instead I stand just beyond her shoulder, my eyes
feeling dry and hot from not blinking. The fryer
is beeping, and behind me, Terry barks my name
telling me to pull the fries. This draws Sarah's eyes.

We look at each other for the first time since April
and probably longer, because even when she
was still masquerading as a friend, her judgment
had boiled, she had begun her silent jury
of my life, never looking me in my eyes.

Even that day at the bus stop,
when she brought down the axe
disguised as piety between us:

*We are two different people and I think
it's better if I pray for you*

from a distance. Right now I need
to unburden my soul before
I can help yours.

We stare at each other through
the drive-thru window, and I wonder
if she's remembering what she said,
the way her words flowed so freely,
not from practice but from ease,
and mine stopped in my throat.

Her mother's in the passenger side,
handing over the money, and Sarah
passes it in to Debbie.

I pull the fries. They're not burnt.
I bag them, pass it to Debbie, silent.
Debbie is about to hand their order
through the window when Sarah
holds up one palm: *Actually*

can we have another order
of fries? That girl wasn't
wearing gloves.

I don't know how it ends.

I turn away and end up in the supply closet.
I am surrounded by industrial-size cans
of condiments and pillars of napkins.
I breathe in the smell of bleach and beef.
I could live here, I think.
I could live right here. I could eat
ketchup and whatever else

and never have to walk
out into the world ever again.

The door opens behind me,
and I turn expecting Debbie.

It's Terry. He's wearing the face
that I've seen on other snouts:
the concern mask. The one
that pretends to be serious,
but behind the serious
is something sparkling.

Did something happen?
Is this because I shouted
at you about the fries?
I'm sorry if I scared you

and his concerned arm
encircles my shoulders,
his frown hovers above my head.

Dear Medusa, I think.
Would you rather be snake
or stone? Would you rather
hurt yourself or everyone
your eye falls upon? Probably
you would rather that
you had never been turned
into a monster
at all.

"Terry, how about you give that girl some goddamn space?"

I didn't think Debbie could curse. She looks like a sitcom
grandmother, neat silver hair and violet eyeglasses
on a chain. When she opens the door
that chain is swinging, and her eyebrows are arched
above the frame. *Can't you see she's upset?*
Why is this door closed? Someone's asking
for the manager up front, and that
would be you, Terry. Alicia, I need your help
taking some things out to the dumpster.

Her voice is like an eagle swinging down
from the highest clouds, talons bared
and driven by the weight of wing
and gravity, strong enough to make
a wolf spring back, severe enough
to make the fangs abandon prey.

Terry leaves fast. It's just me
and Debbie and the fast-approaching
army of my tears, and she either
doesn't see, or pretends not to,
but she tugs on my sleeve
and gestures for me to follow
out the back door.

We carry armfuls of everything expired

Bread and produce and turnovers
piled into boxes, and it's all supposed to go
straight into the dumpster. I know this

because I've done it, and I move to rip
open the bags, toss it all straight in,
but Debbie stops my hand, shakes her head.

Terry tells us to take it out of the packaging
so that homeless people can't eat it,
but Terry has never been hungry
and I don't know what heaven
he thinks he's getting into
by dumping bread into mud
but me and him must think
about different gods
when we pray.

And she shows me the other side
of the dumpster, between the metal
and the wall, where she stacks
everything in a neat pile,
the bread and the tomatoes
and the heads of lettuce
that faceless corporate bosses
say is no longer good enough for customers.

She piles it all up nicely and then leans
against the wall to smoke
a cigarette, waves at me to stand back.

You're so young, she says.
Your lungs are still pink and clean.
Sometimes it's hard to remember
that you and your body
are in this together.
But try not to forget.

Also, do me a favor, honey:
quit this job and do something
else with your precious time.

You're sixteen.
I know it's not all sweet
but hang in there.

Hang in there.

I'm not even sure what it's supposed to mean.
It's a slogan that has always been printed
under the photo of a cat hanging from a branch
or the coyote hanging from the ledge.

Hang in there implies help
is coming, but I don't hear any sirens.

Then again, maybe some help
walks on silent feet:

Debbie in the doorway
when Terry's palm closed on my shoulder;
Deja's whispers in ISAP;
Mr. West and his razor blade;
Dr. Kareem and Medusa;
Geneva
Geneva
Geneva

In the old days when a cat was stuck
in a tree they would call the fire department.
Now there are too many things on fire
to waste time on one little cat.

Surely they get down on their own
eventually? Surely they realize
the strength of their claws
and climb.

Letter to Medusa: Part 3

How does it feel to know
that after the boy with all the gifts,
all those blessings,

came and took your head,
that he used your dead eyes
to vanquish his enemies,

took the only monstrous gift
you were ever given
and made it his own weapon?

Hey Poseidon

I always hear how your brother
Zeus liked to turn into animals
to walk the earth and have his way
with women:

bull
swan
cuckoo

Did you ever take a page
from that godly book

Did you ever set foot
as paw

Did you ever go gray
and running

Did you even bother
to pretend
to be any other predator
than the one you
already are?

At home I think I'm alone

but when I'm closing the microwave on my leftovers
I hear the rise and fall of laughter in the basement,
my brother and his friends
playing a game or watching a movie.

I hurry with my food, hoping I can eat
and disappear before they come upstairs,
but I am just putting my plate in the dishwasher
when the basement door opens,
the sound of feet up the steps,
the smell of cat and weed rising.

Justin appears first, mid-conversation:

I'd never fuck a Black girl, he's saying,
*but the girl in that movie could make me
think about it,*

and my brother and the other two boys
Cody and Andrew, or Cliff, or Coby,
all laugh, and they all smell like smoke
and I wonder if my brother has ever

bothered to tell them that they can't
smoke inside our house, or if his sister
is the only human he has no problem
talking shit to. I ignore them all,

stare only at David. He is the only one
whose shame I am interested in,
whose decline I have watched
from inside the test tube.

Are you going to say anything?
Are you going to tell him he's racist?
I say, and they all look surprised,
as if a mannequin at Target
opened its plaster lips. I squeeze
my glass of water tighter. *Are you*
going to tell them you weren't raised
to talk about people like that?

And David blushes, as if the reminder
of who he used to be is a joke
at his expense, a stain on his pants.
Justin says:

Don't you have a dick to suck?

and laughs, and my brother mumbles
something that sounds like *Shut the fuck*
up, but it's too quiet to hear and too soft
to know
at whom
the words
are aimed.

Hang in there: Part 2

Hang in there, cat,
because there are wolves below,

and although there is kin
on the branch beside you

you can't count on anyone
to pull you up

but
   yourself.

I follow them out into the yard

It's dark. Late. I imagine my mom down the block
staring through her windshield, but no,
she would only do that when the person
being watched is me. We are alone in the night,
the street asleep on a Thursday evening.

My blood is full of wasps.

I'm still clutching the glass of water
and it sloshes over onto my knuckles
as I stride across the grass,
up behind the group,
my legs as shaky and strong
as they are before a track meet.

Hey motherfucker, I say,
and maybe I scream it,
and I watch my foot rise
from the stiff grass

302

and connect with the back
of Justin's knee.

He stumbles forward,
and I meant to throw
the water in his face
but instead I throw
the whole glass
and it cracks into his jaw
as he turns to look
at me. The glass doesn't break

until it hits the ground,
bouncing onto the sidewalk,
and then I launch myself
at him, imagining my hair
streaming like snakes
as red as a comet
    the Big Bang
fucking up his whole world.

He hits me, his arm longer
than I expected, and stronger,
and my own world explodes in stars
but I stay standing long enough
to watch David headbutt
Justin in the stomach,
send him crashing to the ground

where he delivers fist after fist
into his best friend's
face.

No one calls the police.

All of the boys (and me) are white
so although there are eyes
peeking between blinds,
the only thing that happens is Mr. Perry
across the street calling, *You boys
go on home now, you hear!*

They do. Justin limping,
the other boys muttering,
shaking their heads.
One of them calls something
when they're halfway down
the street to which David
shouts, *Bite me, bitch*

and then it's only me and David
in the yard just outside
the aura of the porchlight,
him glancing at me sideways
and muttering
You're so fucking stupid.

Texts with Geneva at midnight

Alicia: I hit a boy in the face today
Geneva: Are you okay?
Alicia: I hit him and you're asking me if I'm okay!
Geneva: I'm assuming he hit you back
Alicia: How did you know?
Geneva: Does a bear shit in the woods?

Geneva: Does a tiger have stripes?

Geneva: Does a wolf howl at the moon?

Alicia: What do you know about wolves

Geneva: Everybody knows about wolves

FRIDAY, JANUARY 25
Letter to Medusa: Part 4

How did you get ready for your day?
Did you brush your fangs,
pet the snakes growing from your scalp,
nod to their hissing like the radio?

Did you eventually get used to
the gray walls of your cavern
or did you ever look toward
the light and think

I want to see the sunset
even if I turn the whole
world to stone?

When Justin hit me

I ducked just enough for his fist
to strike my head.

The tender lump is hidden
under my hair.

Just like
everything else,

the snakes
obscure

the
story.

My mother almost gets me sent to ISAP

when she texts me during Mr. Mattson's class—
luckily he doesn't hate me as much as Mrs. Fisher.

I glance at the text by my locker: *Don't forget
you have an appointment with the eye doctor
this afternoon. I'll take you.*

I write back *okay*
but I'd already been looking at my glasses
on the counter of my bathroom.

I only wear them at night
but there's nothing stopping me now
from wearing them all the time:

no track to run
no burpees to knock
them off my face

In my skull are the same eyes
but my life dictates how they see.

I've been dreading Dr. Kareem's group,

dreading my own mouth, which more and more
I can't seem to keep shut. When we all are assembled
in the music room it's awkward, because usually
Dr. Kareem addresses us as a group, says something
to get a conversation started. Today she just sits
and stares, and stares, and stares, and it's like
sitting in the presence of a great wise owl
and as the time ticks by you can't tell
if you're an owl too or if you're slowly transforming
into a mouse.

I am always thinking of who is the predator,
and who is the prey. I wonder if it will always
be this way, or if eventually I can walk
through the world not as rabbit
or mouse
or even monster
but as a creature
that could eventually
be human.

"I googled hymens"

Eugenia says out of the blue, *what a scam*
and almost everybody laughs, even Dr. Kareem,
but Blake frowns.

> *How is it a scam? Just because people aren't as serious*
> *about virginity as they used to be*
> *doesn't mean that it's fake.*

Dr. Kareem's laugh dwindles away
and Blake, cool-popular-sunflower-
Blake blushes under her gaze
which is never fierce yet
always intense. But Eugenia
answers first:

I mean, prove that it's real though?
I read that some people's hymens
are like a dot, and some people's
are like a ring around the edge.
When they say you lose *your virginity,*
they're saying something is lost.
I don't feel like I lost anything.

Blake stares.
    Okay but it hurts
    the first time. That's
    virginity. That's something.

Then Dr. Kareem speaks up:

Are you speaking from personal
experience?

Blake's only answer
is a blush, so Dr. Kareem goes on.

That one's first time having penetrative sex
must always be very painful is another
myth. I ask you all to always think about
    the production of knowledge:
who makes it,
and for whom.

How can virginity be defined by a hymen
when not every person has one? When no hymen looks
the same? When it can be torn
by horseback, by bicycle, by tampon?

When we are born into this world,
we can scream and we can swallow,
and that's about all. The hymen
is not about chastity, some pristine
bow tied around a wedding-night sacrifice.
It is a gift from nature, to keep bacteria
out of the body we are not yet capable
of caring for without help.
Have you ever changed
a diaper, for god's sake?

Laughter. Even Blake, whose face
is no longer gold sunflower
but red tulip. Dr. Kareem shakes
her head and sighs, finishes:

People, all I'm trying to say
is that if your first time hurts
maybe it's because your hymen
is intact, or maybe it's because
you're nervous and in need
of lubrication.

Either way, please remember
     the production of knowledge
and what we generally accept
as true. Is it a fact, or is it
an electric fence around the yard

to keep the house cat
from exploring the wonders
of the world beyond?

Lena says

I've been thinking,
about what Dr. Kareem said about weapons
created to harm us. And it reminded me of the Bible,
how they say "no weapon formed against me
shall prosper" but I was thinking
that if all these things we talked about
    periods
    and body-shaming
    and hormones
    and gender roles or whatever
    and racism
    and slut-shaming
if these are all weapons formed against
us
then we're helping them prosper
when we turn them
against
each other.

"And what about virgin-shaming?"

Prya says.
Because that's a thing too.

People have sex when they're ready
but everybody is always judging
when *they do it:*

too soon, too late—
everyone always has something
to say. There was a whole movement
about sexual liberation
but we're still on the same old, same old.

A few months ago
I would have heard her
and seen nothing missing

but now, I look at Deja
and I see she's already thinking
the same thing—two options,
nothing in between or beyond.

I open my mouth to speak
up for her, but Deja is already
speaking up for herself:

The thing that bugs me about virginity
is that everyone seems to think being a virgin
means you're saving sex—for God, for prom,
for the right person at the right time.

But I'm not saving it. Why don't people see
that sex is not part of my reality?
Maybe this is like describing the color orange
to eyes that only see black and white

but it's not about purity, it's not about fear
or pain or judgment or God
it's about me and the world that exists
inside me, and sex
is not part of that world,

and it would be great
it would be so freaking great
if people stopped talking about liberation
like it begins and ends
with the decision of when
and where and how
someone says yes *to sex,*
like no *is always temporary*
or a placeholder.

I've been so used
to debate, that who I am
has become a subject on a stage
but I think I am done
debating my reality.

I refuse to let anybody
shrink who I am down to purity.

I'm not sex or abstinence
I'm not a nun or a bride
I'm not clean I'm not dirty
I'm Deja Duvall.

"Well, damn."

For a moment this is all Dr. Kareem says
and then her look of surprise
cracks into a smile and she laughs:

You just exposed a gap in my thinking and I'm grateful. I will have to
    think
about this before I can give a worthy response.

I don't think I've ever heard a teacher react like that
when they were told something they didn't know.

I will say, she adds,
the word slut-shaming
assumes there is a slut to shame.
As I've said before,
there is no such thing as a slut,
a whore, a hoe. There are only people
who choose to have sex
and those who choose not to—
she looks at Deja—*either*
temporarily or not!
The number of partners
is irrelevant.
We are not who we have sex with
We are not who we don't have sex with.

We are an expanse.

And I hear her, and it should probably
make me feel better, but in my head
all I can think about is the word
CHOOSE
and the echo of its binary.

Choose. Or choose not.
In so many cases
I can't find myself
in these two categories.

I have gotten into cars, stepped
through doorways, and didn't want
to be there. But my feet walked,

my waist bent to sit.
I was not duct-taped.
I was not handcuffed in a trunk.
And still, in the back of my mind,
I felt that many things were before me
but choice wasn't one of them.

What choice does a rabbit have
walking through a world of wolves?
Does the rabbit have to grow fangs
to survive, or does it have to recognize
its softness and transform?

Why can't a rabbit be a rabbit?
Why am I comparing women
    to rabbits
        to begin with?

I think again of what Deja said:
circle, heart, box.

What Dr. Kareem said
about electric fences.

Maybe I don't feel free
because I haven't yet
run
far enough.

"You said there's no such thing as a slut,"

Prya says. She's still grappling.
We all are.

But if there's
no such thing
as a virgin
either, then
what is there?

And Dr. Kareem
grins like
Prya has dug
her hands deep
into dark
soil and
found gold.

Dr. Kareem spends the rest of the group listening

to everyone talk about ways we can be in partnership
with other women and spends five minutes
facilitating a debate between Lena and Annika
when Annika says trans girls need their own
partnership instead of expecting sisterhood
from cis girls. I recognize myself in Lena,
the desire to be silent battling with the flame
that builds in your belly and struggles
up your throat. There are things
that are important to one person, things
that we feel need to be important
to everyone. This is how the world
works, this is how the world continues
to turn, and maybe
get better.

Lena's argument

Annika is saying only a cis girl
has experienced
the struggle of
girlhood and womanhood
like your *girlhood*
your *womanhood* is the same
as everyone else's
in this room

> like Deja's girlhood
> is the same as mine
> or mine is the same
> as Alicia's.

> Prya
has to fight every day
to persuade these teachers
to give Muslim students the
respect that they give
Christian kids at this
dumbass school,

> Deja
has to spend her girlhood
educating adults
on why her girlhood
matters, so why

> is a trans girl's

girlhood
　　her coming
　　　　of age

any different, why
is her experience
of girlhood not just
another facet on the
diamond of woman

why can't we all just
　　shine together

Deja says

because diamonds' value is inflated
by an exploitive structure
that assigns worth based on
an arbitrary set of rules

and Dr. Kareem says

Sounds about right

and we all laugh
even me, and I'm so proud
to have a best friend
who can make a joke
like that, even while
people's eyes are full
of tears.

Texts with Deja

Deja: I always feel like I can punch a hole in the sky after Dr.
Kareem's group

Alicia: Or punch a hole in someone's face

Deja: Whose? Anyone specific?

Alicia: I can think of a few.

Alicia: can I ask you something?

Deja: of course

Alicia: I probably should have asked you this before. How did it
make you feel when we talked about sex in the group before
today? With you being asexual?

Deja: Invisible.

Alicia: I thought it might

Deja: I'm torn. Cuz on one hand everyone notices that I'm Black right
away . . . it feels nice to have part of who I am be hide-able. But
people just assume that all girls are available for sex and it's just
a matter of persuasion and damn I just wanna live and BE on my
own terms.

Alicia: praise hands.gif

Deja: ew don't lol

Alicia: sorry

The diamond of woman

I don't much feel like a diamond but I can't get
Lena's speech about girlhood out
of my mind. My girlhood
      isn't Deja's
      isn't Lena's

318

isn't Prya's
isn't Eugenia's
isn't Annika's

but we are like the Olympic rings,
Venn diagrams with corners
of our lives overlapping. We have
so many things in common,
chief among them
wolves

and it's disappointing
no, upsetting
no, enraging

that of all the things we have in common
the one we feel deepest is that we've all been bitten
by the same set of fangs
or at the very least
seen them flashing
from the dark.

"Be there in ten minutes"

texts my mother, and I'm thinking about the puff
of air they whiff into your eyeball at the optometrist
while I make my way toward my locker.

I'm five feet away by the time I notice
the piece of paper sticking out
of the grille, waving softly
in the breeze of passing students.

I freeze. I don't want to go any closer:
the white paper is a crime scene
is a contagion zone
is a glowing SOS

Touching it feels like stepping in blood
tracking it all over the house
then wondering which puddles
are mine
or hers.

The note:

I need to talk
to you. Meet me
in the library
after school

I sit down next to my mother and she asks why I'm sweating

I ran from my locker.
It's the truth.
I did.
I just don't tell her
that what I'm running from
is handwriting written
in blue loops,
words from a grave
dug behind
a closed door.

I barely notice the puff of air

I read the letters

E

F P

T O Z

L P E D

I compare slides:
    The first one is better
    than the second one
    Okay, now the second one
    looks better

I'm always afraid I'm failing a test
when the only test to fail here
is truth. Can you read line five
or not? Two options.

Can you see what's in front of you?
Are you afraid to admit
when things get blurry?

They recommend new lenses for my glasses

even though my mother says I don't wear them,
and in my head I'm still hearing my own frail whisper:
    You can wear glasses now. You don't run.
But Mom is oblivious. Says yes to new contacts,
and the doctor's assistant leads me over to the mirrored
section where I'm supposed to put the new lenses
into my eyeball and demonstrate that they fit,
they work, they allow me to see.

Once they're in, I see.
I see him.

The same doctor from last year,
his neat haircut, his tie, his white
coat, his smooth beard. His hands.

Let's make sure these look all right,
he says, and he settles down across
from me, studying each eye.
Underneath the desk, our knees
touch. My mother is on her phone
several yards away, waiting for me,
no need to watch. Plain sight.

And it's not as if he has his palm
down or up
my shirt, it's not as if he's
the guy on the bus with his dick
in his hand, but his fingers
are against my cheeks, and his face
is inches away, and from a distance
one would think he's just doing
his job, but his knees are against
my knees, and in the center
of each of his eyes there is a sparkle
like a fleck of gold sinking into a muddy river.

None of this makes me bleed. None of this
is something that, alone, I couldn't bear.
But everything seems to be bleeding together,
and carried along on the current

are white pieces of paper sticking out of my locker
screaming ME TOO
and yes, maybe I could bear it all, bear this . . .
but after everything else
    why should I
    why should I
    why should I

My eyes are already open but now
I open my mouth, wondering
if I'm brave enough
to scream.

"What the fuck do you think you're doing?"

I jump, and so does he. It takes me five seconds
to fully realize that it wasn't my voice
but my mother's,

that she is standing two feet away
with her face contorted in rage,

that she is pointing at the eye doctor
that he has pushed away from the desk
that my knees are cooling like rain on scorched earth
that his mouth is half-open
that he is stammering excuses
that my mother goes on shouting
that other women have come to look
that most of the men stay in their seats
that two of the assistants are looking wise
that one of them shakes her head

that I'm only wearing one contact
that the room is blurry
that my mother goes on shouting
that my mother has one hand on my shoulder
that my mother goes on shouting
that she is pulling me away from the desk
that she is telling him "I saw you, I saw you"
that my mother goes on shouting
that my mother goes on shouting
that my mother goes on shouting
that he disappears into the back room

it takes me thirty minutes to stop crying
it takes me an hour to tell her she was right
it takes me until midnight to realize my mother
    saved me from a wolf

Politeness is a trap

One year I had to do CPR and safety training
for babysitter training. I learned
to breathe into the lungs, to pump
the chest, to clench my fists
beneath the diaphragm to dislodge
food from the windpipe.

The trainer cautioned us
about women who choke:
    Women are raised
    to never make a scene.
    They start to choke

at a restaurant, and excuse
themselves to the bathroom
so as not to disturb
the other diners,
and they die
on the floor
alone

and thinking about this
it occurs to me
that the only reason the eye doctor
gets away with it
is because in such a public place
he is counting on the rabbits
we were raised to be.

Our politeness is prey,
mice
that don't
squeak.

Turtles

don't trust the world with their softness—
after who knows how many eons
of learning this the hard way
a shell grew from their flesh,
dappled with the colors of forest:
double defense.

I don't remember when my mother
started calling me Turtle.

I'm reminded that she has known me
longer than anyone, that she might know
how long I've been soft and scared
before my memory even begins

and that even through the crack
of my shell
she might see me
once she knows where
to look.

Texts with Geneva

Alicia: Are you out of the closet to your mom

Geneva: No. Well, kinda. I just assume she knows.

Alicia: What's stopping you from just telling her?

Geneva: Good question. Maybe I just don't feel like explaining things right now. Or maybe I wouldn't have to explain at all. I don't know.

Alicia: Do you ever feel like if you have to balance one more thing on your head, everything will come crashing down

Geneva: Sometimes. But you know what the answer is when you feel like that?

Alicia: No

Geneva: Handing something to someone to hold ;)

Alicia: I don't think your hands are big enough

Geneva: Then maybe we can just put it down

Alicia: Or burn it

Geneva: Burning it is always an option

Thoughts about Geneva

At camp when I kissed Renée, the whole cabin
felt like a glowing universe
shrunk down around us,
everything so simultaneously huge and tiny
that I could fit myself in my own pocket.

I know everyone imagines bi girls
as just trying to get attention
from guys

and bi boys are supposedly
just apprehensive about saying
they're "fully gay"

but I can't help but think that both
of these scenarios
make it seem like men
are at the center of everyone's attraction

and maybe sometimes they are
but in this small universe of my heart
Geneva is the sun
and I am
every revolving planet.

MONDAY, JANUARY 28
I'm standing in the kitchen shoving all my papers

into my bag. I'm wearing my last pair
of contacts. They will last five days
and then it will be time to slip on
the glasses. But for now, the world
looks clear, if not bright.

My mother walks in, and then my brother
and for a moment
we are all standing silently
in the same room, three
pairs of the same cheekbones
and the same wide mouths
frowning for the same
and different reasons.

Did you get in a fight?
she says to my brother.
This is the first time she has seen him
since he hit Justin, the slight bruise
under his eye more like a lilac kiss by now.
David and I exchange glances.

No, he says. *Just fucking around
with Justin.*

Oh you two are still friends?
I say, here under the safety
of my mother's gaze.

He puts on his jacket.
I can't make him answer.
I can only let my eyes
follow him out the door,
hoping he feels them
long after he's out
of sight.

I put on khakis with no stain

My mother has slipped new clothes into my closet
the same size and brand as what I was wearing
before, the tags still on and no grease
spot by the knee. You're supposed to wash

new clothes before you wear them,
but I slip them on and stare down
at the smooth clean fabric, surprised
by the way the spotlessness
makes me feel
new too.

The bus is late and so am I

so everyone is already in class by the time I arrive,
stopping by the office for a tardy slip.
They know my face by now, raise eyebrows
meant to warn me about their judgment
but I only raise my eyebrow back, because
none of them have ever actually talked to me
and yet my name on pink slips of paper,
passed on by Mrs. Fisher, gives them a story
to hear, and then repeat. I take my slip and go.

I have to pass Hall 1 for my own first class,
and I'm crossing an open door when I hear
voices raised coming from inside:

Miss Duvall, I have asked you repeatedly
not to wear gang colors in your jewelry.

329

It specifically violates the handbook
and the spirit of our school.

It's Mrs. Bullock and she's talking
to Deja. I pause, feeling all
my bones turning into metal birds,
fluttering and sinking simultaneously.

It's an AIDS awareness wristband, Mrs. Bullock.

It's a gang color that violates
the student handbook, Miss Duvall.

Deja is calm but Mrs. Bullock's voice
sharpens and soars. *One day*
it won't be security that comes to get you
but the police!

And then I'm in the classroom.

Everyone is blinking at me, including
Deja, trying to figure out
what I'm doing there. I don't know
either, only that the mouth I can
no longer rely upon to stay closed
is open and speaking to Mrs. Bullock:

What kind of fucking teacher are you
Let's look at everything red in your classroom
Adam's shoelaces, your lipstick,
Jill's backpack, Hannah's nails.
Are they all going to ISAP?
Look at my fucking hair.
Am I?

Answer: yes

Me and Deja walk side by side
behind Mr. Upton, who shakes
his head while he walks.

*Ricky ain't gonna believe
this shit,* he says.

Who's Ricky? says Deja.

Mr. West.

. . . Ricky West, I whisper.

Is he a DJ? Deja mutters.

You two shut up, Mr. Upton says,
but he's chuckling
when he says it.

After Mr. Ricky West chews us out

while Mr. Upton laughs, we settle into desks
and listen to Marvin Gaye and Tammi Terrell
sing about pictures in a frame. I've never
been in ISAP this early, barely a quarter
of the way through first period.

Mr. West, I say after a while.
Can I go to my locker?
I don't even have my books.

He gives me a long stare,
an uncle look, and gives me a hall pass,

with a face that says
Don't try any bullshit,
and I nod and nod and nod.

The halls are empty, and with the orange
pass in my hand, I feel like I've been given
a ticket to the moon, to Mars, free
to roam. But I come sinking down
to Earth when I get to my hallway
and see the white paper
emerging from my locker.

The note

*I'm going to report him.
But I want to talk to you
first. Meet me after school.
library. By Poe.*

My feet carry me to the Colonel's hallway

to his always-open door, propped open now
with an ancient brown doorstop. He has a class:
I can hear him talking about mitochondria,
the same jokes he's always told making his voice
light, making him the teacher everyone
wishes their other teachers were like.

The Colonel
    is an alibi for himself.
    is paint over asbestos
    is a pothole patched with gum

I stare down at my clean, new khakis,
the way the angle of the lights casts
shadows like stains down the front.

These won't always be my pants, but these
will always be my legs.

These will always be my legs
These will always be my legs
These will always be mine

I would've been in art class

and I peek in, watch Geneva's brush rising and sinking
rising and sinking, a face appearing before her.

I watch until it takes shape:
     the ironic eyebrows
     the almost-crooked nose
     the all-knowing grin

her father, emerging from the white canvas,
the pieces of him she takes with her
everywhere she goes.

I text her: *You have your dad's smile*
and wait just long enough
to watch her peek at her phone,
for that smile to tinge her mouth,
before I disappear back down
the hall.

Texts with Stephanie from Meat Palace

Alicia: I'm going to be a little late today, I'm sorry. Something I have to do after school.

Stephanie: That's okay. I've got Debbie and Rodney and Forrest working.

Alicia: Not Terry?

Stephanie: Nope.

Stephanie: Btw he got chewed out by the regional boss last week

Alicia: Why?

Stephanie: Who knows. Sounded like a customer filed a complaint.

Alicia: A deep-fried mystery

Stephanie: He's a deep-fried asshole

Stephanie: Delete that 😊

Geneva is at my locker after school

I'd rather see her waiting there than another wavering
piece of white paper. She thinks she's walking me to work
and I can't think of a way to tell her or not tell her
without sounding shadier than I feel.

I have to meet someone after school,
I say. *It's important.*

Her face that always knows everything
does not know this. I've never seen her frown
except when she's concentrating.

Can I text you after? I say.

Will you?

Yes. Is that okay?

It's going to have to be, isn't it?

I can feel me pushing her too far.
I want to grab her back and hold her.

But I watch her leave, watch everyone leave,
waiting for the crowds to clear, for
the eyes to disappear. The library
is never busy after school
or even during school.

The portrait of Edgar Allan Poe
on the back wall is a place
where teachers tell us to meet
when we have research projects.

This is not a research project.
I don't know what this is.

All I know is that whoever's hand
writes in blue loops that look like the path
of a robin's wings, wrote the words
Me too,
that they have stood on the closed side
of an always-open door
and somehow they know
that I have too.

Edgar Allan Poe isn't the only face on the walls

Octavia Butler is painted by the checkout desk,
Margaret Atwood by her side. Toni Morrison
and Sonia Sanchez, who I know from the poetry anthology
I stole from my brother when we were kids.

With no distractions, it's easy to look around
this place, at all the painted portraits,

and tell myself I'm seeing it for the first time,
notice all the details that I've missed in the three
years I've been a student at Marshall.

I've never noticed the portrait of Herman Melville
wearing a shirt that says *I luv whales*
or the smiling face of Jane Austen
holding a sign that reads *gossip belongs in literature.*

All these stories, all these faces—
it takes me a moment to realize
when a real face has appeared beside me,
to realize that the penny-bright hair
the freckled skin,
the deep deep frown
belong to Blake Felipe.

"You finally came."

Inside my backpack, all the notes from my locker
feel as if they've suddenly caught fire, burning
a hole through the fabric. It's not until now

that I realize how hard I was trying not
to imagine who the notes were from.

No name meant no face, no face
meant not real.

I have spent so much of the last year
wishing nothing were real,
but everything is

and I can tell by the look in Blake's
eyes that she has been trapped inside

a wolf's jaws
and now she's clawing
toward the sun.

We end up outside

and we both say at the same time
Spring will be here soon.
Tomorrrow it will be March.
Track season officially starts.
Spring break.
Prom gossip.

I want to skip it all.

It's almost been a year, says Blake,
and all the wandering my brain
does when it's free-falling,
when it's looking for a soft place
to land, comes to a stop.

I saw you on April fourth. With him.
After school. I saw you walk in,
I saw the door close. I know
what the closed door means.
It was April seventh for me.
The year before.
Was that the first time?

No. I think it started
in March.

I hate the spring, she says.

Her voice is a well,
the echoes long and deep.
She is pulling her ribs
out through her mouth
one by one
and all I can do is listen
and sit
and cry.

Blake Felipe is a perfect girl.

She has had the same boyfriend since freshman year.
She never breaks dress code.
She always buttons the top button of her uniform.
She always turns in her homework.
She smiles in her yearbook photo.
She gets elected to homecoming court.
She always wears clean shoes.
She always smiles and nods.
She always has a pack of girls surrounding her.
She always laughs at their jokes.
She never raises her voice.

Blake Felipe is a perfect girl
she stands as close to the center
of the box as she can get
and for all the talk about what I wore
and who I took off my bra for,
in the end, we are the same.

It started sophomore year

then kept going.
Blake is a senior.
She has been going to this school
    year after year
smiling her way toward graduation

and no one—
    not even her boyfriend—
knows what
she's been
smiling
through.

Blake says

I decided I'm going to tell the cops.
It's almost the science fair
and he always gives his speeches
and takes pictures with the trophies
and does his whole act.

I'm telling,
but I couldn't tell until
I talked to you and told you
that I'm sorry I didn't warn
you, that I'm sorry I didn't
scream fire *the very first time.*

I'm going to tell them
there are other girls

I'm going to tell them I saw
I'm going to tell them I know
I'm going to tell them it's him
I'm going to tell them it's all
    too late

but that I'm graduating soon
and then I'll be free of him
    this place
    these walls
    these bricks

this school
    that feels like a grave
    that feels like a slaughterhouse
    that feels like a place to drown

A car appears before us

Red Chevrolet, a blaze so bright it looks wet
in the gray spring fog. Devin, her boyfriend,
with his head out the window shouting
    Let's roll!
and I watch her face transform
the mask rising out of the ash
bright and convincing.

I am sitting beside
    the homecoming queen
    the field hockey champion
    the honor roll student
    the good girlfriend

the honest daughter
a human

She has not dyed her hair red,
but inside her everything is burning
everything is burning down
and down
and down

I walk to work alone, thinking

about how the Colonel is also burning—
he was the scorching match.

I wonder how many girls he set ablaze
who left this place seemingly whole
only to burn down later, away,
where the sparks couldn't catch.

Blake has been smoldering but her plan
is to take her fiery hands and cup them
around the entire school before she goes

and then she will graduate and be gone
but I
will still
be here.

Texts with Blake

Alicia: Was it after school for you too
Blake: Yes
Alicia: How long in between

Blake: Sometimes a week. Sometimes a month

Alicia: Me too

Blake: Did he ever apologize

Alicia: Yes. But then he did it again

Blake: Me too

Alicia: Did he ever call you to his class and not do it

Blake: Yes. Asked me to help him grade papers or clean up

Alicia: Me too

Blake: Did you ever think you were crazy, maybe you just
     imagined it

Alicia: Yes

Blake: Me too

Alicia: Does it make you . . . mad? Sad? That everyone loves him?

Blake: Yes.

Alicia: Me too

Blake: Did you ever try to tell your parents

Alicia: Yes.

Blake: Me too

Alicia: Did you think if you could just make it through that you'd just
     leave, graduate, and forget

Me too me too me too me too me too me too me too me too me
     too me too me too me too me too me too me too me too me
     too me too me too me too me too me too

Meat Palace and randoms are in the same box

in my head: autopilot, no thinking
just doing, just hands working,
wearing two different uniforms.

But today while I make change
and feed the hungry
I can't turn my brain off

I can't disconnect my hands
from myself, can't shove everything
away into boxes—the lids are open
and everything overlaps:
    all the girls I used to be
    all the girls I have been
    all the girls I am

are customers zooming through drive-thru

and they have been hungry for as long
as I can remember—
aren't we all hungry for something?
I am allowed to be hungry.

Hunger

I have been looking at every late night, every step into moonlight,
    every slip of cotton and nylon as
a path springing from the Colonel, from Adam in the park and my
    silent scream

but the only path leads from myself to myself:

me hungry, me curious, me wild, me trying to kiss my way back
    toward the wonder of touch

toward skin and not biblical flesh

I have been told that girls like me are hurting, that girls who have
    explored this many backseats are in pain

and I am
    I am

but I am healing too

there are states between hurting and healing

    I walk in that space

I am trying to hold on to my body

I am finding my way

Texts with Blake

Alicia: do you think every girl who sleeps with a lot of guys has . . .
    "problems"?

Blake: no. I know girls who just like to have a lot of sex. My sister's
    in college and she hooks up with everybody just because she
    feels like it.

Alicia: so you really don't think sluts exist, like Dr. Kareem said

Blake: I think I need to figure out what to think. Production of
    knowledge, remember?

Alicia: no offense but I think you'd figure out what to think if people
    had been calling you a whore all year

Blake: fair

Alicia: I've spent all this time wanting to be you

Blake: you can't be

Alicia: why not

Blake: because you're you

Alicia: and who are you?

Blake: I didn't stay with Devin this whole time because I love him. I kept dating him because having a boyfriend makes me feel safer

Alicia: do you ever wish you did things just because you want to do them, and not because the Colonel did what he did

Blake: yes

Alicia: me too

Texts with Blake

Alicia: How did you know? About me?

Blake: You look on the outside how I feel on the inside. One day I was walking to calc. I saw you go in. I saw the door close.

Alicia: Why didn't you say something before? To me

Blake: You know what it means to pretend, right?

Alicia: Yes

Blake: Me too

Alicia: I've seen the door closed too. Was that you? This year?

Blake: Yes. But maybe someone else too.

Alicia: He called me to his office a couple weeks ago. Called Mrs. Fisher and had her send me.

Blake: I'm sorry

Alicia: He's not going to stop, is he

Blake: No

Letter to Medusa: Part 5

You never had a curly fry
but if you ever got the chance
to stand over the boiling pit
of a modern fryer, you would probably
have done what I did:

poured everything in,

bag after bag
fries
mozzarella sticks
chicken

watched it all turn black

mozzarella sticks turning into charred shipwrecks

fries like a crumbled house

Rodney calls Stephanie and, god
bless her, she doesn't scream at me,
just holds me by the shoulders
and says, *You should probably
go home.*

So I do.

Text from a random

Him: I think I just saw you walking down Vine. Want a ride?

Alicia: Do you know how old I am

Him: ?

Alicia: How old are you?

Him: Why does that matter?

Alicia: I want to know how old you are

Him: Age is just a number 😊

Alicia: Age is life, age is experience, age is a car, age is money, age is voting, age is rights, age is an entire system, age is power. It's more than a number

Him:

Alicia: ????

Him:

These shoes aren't made for running

but I run anyway. The ground is wet and the trees
are coming back to life but all I can smell
is the burning fries at Meat Palace, the odor
of smoke joining with grease, the way
everything turned slippery and hot.

My new pants are ruined, machine-gunned
with spots of grease. I did this to myself.
It's like everything that makes me feel
unclean has no choice but to rise
out of me and appear on my clothes
and on my skin. It doesn't matter
what I wear: inside the cloth

is still this body, and no matter
how many showers I take
how much I exfoliate
I can't rinse off the thing
that clings to me.

But I'm running.
I have not run far enough.
I have to keep running
until I break through
that electric shock

Dirty or not
damaged or not
I am flying
My feet are my wings
Are my
Are mine

Fuck you, Poseidon, and you too, Athena, and you too, Hera,

and you too, Perseus, you bitch.
You needed golden
sandals to do
what I do.

You took
a sword   and a shield   and a cloak
and those
shoes

and you thought
it made you
a god
because
you spilled
the blood
that everyone
whispered
about spilling.

You killed Medusa
and then married
Andromeda, and you
probably thought
she was so different
because she was naked
and helpless when you
rescued her. But

what you don't know
is that Medusa was once naked
and helpless too,

and that you and all
the gods and goddesses
spent lifetimes
convincing everyone
that Medusa was
a monster, when
the slightest change
in story
could have given
Andromeda
the snakes.

While I run, I think of swords

It's easy to behead the monster
with so many gods providing the tools

but what if Medusa wants
Poseidon's head
on a plate

what if Medusa wants
her own temple
with Athena
barred for life?

What if Medusa
has her own ideas
about justice
and they don't
just stop
with Perseus?

I arrive sweating in the kitchen

just as my mother puts the voicemail
from her phone on speaker.

This message is for the parents of Alicia Rivers—

and all the adrenaline that carried me
from Meat Palace to the door surges one more time,
propelling me across the kitchen to try
to intercept her hand, erase it before
she knows what she's hearing. But
the words are out, and she stares at me,
the voice entering our ears together,
not who I expected:

This is Coach Tinsley at Marshall
High School. I wanted to see
if we could talk about Alicia
and get her more involved
in extracurriculars. She needs
more credits to graduate
and I know she's been having
some trouble this year
but maybe we can get her
on the right track. That pun
was unintentional, my apologies.
Give me a call back when . . .

My mother has lifted her eyes
from the machine and studies me
with a growing frown.

What trouble does he mean?
You're not running track
anymore? What happened?

I don't tell her the truth.
It's still a knot in my throat. But
she sees me now:
I recognize her recognition.

She is a hound in the woods
who has caught the scent of wolf.
It's only a matter of time.

Texts with Geneva

Alicia: Are you awake

Geneva: I think we're both night owls. Did you do what you needed to do after school?

Alicia: Yes. Can I ask you something?

Geneva: Yes

Alicia: Do you only like me because I work at Meat Palace?

Geneva: Shut up lol

Alicia: I'm going to quit.

Geneva: There goes my fast-food connect.

Alicia: Maybe my skin will get better away from all that grease

Geneva: I think your skin is beautiful

Alicia: Changing the subject

Geneva: To?

Alicia: You

Geneva: What about me?

Alicia: Who was your first love?

Geneva: Myself

Alicia: Perfect

Texts with Deja

Alicia: I think I'm going to run next Friday

Deja: 🌚

Alicia: Come on

Deja: Do you think you'll be ready? Have you even been conditioning?

Alicia: You have no idea.

Texts with Deja

Deja: btw I finished that book The Color Purple

Alicia: How was it?

Deja: Definitely like poetry. I hate that she got raped though

Alicia: Oh. She did?

Deja: I was thinking about Medusa. Isn't it bullshit how nothing changes in 3,000 years, or even in 100 years.

Alicia: And definitely not in one

Alicia: By the way, did you know Andromeda was actually probably Black

Deja: The most beautiful woman in the world? That tracks

Alicia: I wonder if Mrs. Bullock knows that

Deja: Mrs. Bullock doesn't know her ass from the Odyssey

Texts with Deja

Deja: guess what

Alicia: 👀

Deja: I think I met somebody

Alicia: !!!!

Deja: His name is Farhan.

Alicia: Where did you meet him?

Deja: At debate. We got paired to debate fracking.

Deja: I destroyed him. 😏

Alicia: Of course you did. What's he like?

Deja: He's smart. He's beautiful. He's romantic. He's read Audre Lorde.

Alicia: . . . who's Audre Lorde?

Deja: Jesus Alicia 🙎

Alicia: I'm sorry, I'm googling!

Alicia: Oh I know her. She writes poetry.

Deja: she does??

Alicia: Jesus Deja!

Deja: bye!! lol

Dear David

Last night I had a dream that we were on a sailboat
and the wind blew so hard that the sail
ripped into the sky, and the ocean
around us was a flat gray coin.

We sat on the boat together, quiet,
until I realized both of us were on fire.

And it was weird because my fire
was only burning me, and the smoke
was choking only my lungs,

but your fire was spreading
to the boat and I kept saying
David, watch it, watch it,

but you were just staring
at the sky and burning

and burning
and while I was turning myself
into ash, you were sinking
our boat.

Then there were other boats
all around us, and the sparks
from your flames were catching
their sails, turning the whole ocean
into a flaming orange rage,

and I said David, look, why
can't you just keep it
to yourself? *and when*
I woke up I still didn't know
why I was the one
who felt guilty.

David, I know we're both
on fire, and I have no idea
what lit your blaze
but don't you see
that the way you've chosen
to burn is sinking
all the ships and not just
your own?

I slip it under his door

the way I used to, the way we used to
when we were two sides
of the same coin and not

two foreign currencies
both shimmering down
through murky water.

TUESDAY, MARCH 5
I cross the parking lot at school

and see Blake Felipe climbing out of Devin's
red car. She swings her bag over her shoulder

and now that I know where to look
I see the ghosts under her eyes,

the way her boyfriend's hand on her shoulder
weighs more than he could ever even know.

We lock eyes, only for a moment, and then
her gaze sweeps over the parking lot

at all the people streaming toward
Marshall's pale stones. We are searching

for the same thing: pondering the faces
of our peers and wondering how many

wear our same mask.

Text to Blake

Alicia: Do you ever wonder who you would be if it had never
   happened
Blake: Yes
Alicia: Me too

Any day that's not Friday isn't a day at all

Thursday I go to work and give Terry two weeks' notice.
He says *Sure, fine,* and goes back to shuffling papers,
not looking me in the eye. Debbie is slicing beef
ten feet away, and I feel her eyes even with
her back turned. I come and look over her shoulder

watching her hands move expertly over the machine,
over the meat, her missing finger barely missing.

How long did it take for you to get used to it,
I ask, and she smiles a little.

I don't know if you ever get used to it, she says.
A piece of you is missing. But you get along,
and you learn new ways to live.

But I can't find new ways to live

Can't just go on without my missing piece
Can't just get along

Not when the Colonel
    is still smiling for pictures
    is still wearing wool
    is still howling at the moon
    is still slowly closing his door

What do I do
about the pieces he has taken from others
about all the pieces
he has yet
to take?

Text to Blake

Alicia: Why didn't you tell before?

Blake: There are a lot of reasons.

Alicia: Tell me one?

Blake: You know how every time it comes out that a celebrity or a politician has raped someone or even sexually harassed someone, everyone on social media has an opinion about it? Family, friends, everybody?

Alicia: Yeah

Blake: When you see your aunts and grandfathers and dad and friends all call women liars over and over again, you don't need to wonder if anyone will believe you if you tell.

Alicia: Because they've basically already told you.

Blake: Right.

Alicia: If a man is loved enough, a woman can't be hated enough

Blake: Exactly.

My mother comes in late

and I'm not sleeping
and she must know
because she opens my door
because she sits on the edge of my bed
because she whispers into the dark
because she explains she's trying
because she has been carrying a lot
because some of it she hasn't put down since she was ten
because nothing changes in a hundred years
because wolves are in all the oldest stories
because we have discovered fire but still don't know what to do with it

but my mom says she's trying to learn what to do with it
because she knows I'm going through something
because she's been going to group therapy
because she wants to be there for me
because she knows she hasn't been
because she's been buried
because she's so lonely
and when she lies down
I make room for her
and she doesn't talk
anymore, she just
sleeps and so
do
I.

FRIDAY, MARCH 8
The cafeteria is being set up for the science fair

All the science geeks setting up their presentations.
It's not like movies, where the projects are volcanoes
and rudimentary machines built with coffee cans.

Our science geeks are serious: organ donation research
Perpetual-motion machines
Cloud services for breast cancer diagnosis
Sand bioreactors

Our school always wins trophies
and the faces in the setup are focused,
ignoring everyone not affiliated with the fair.

Today is also the first track meet
and Jacob and Tierra

and the other runners cluster
in the halls between classes,
pacing like tigers,
prickly and electric.

Part of me wants to cross the chasm,
tell them I'll be there beside them
at the starting line. But every time

I pass the cafeteria I see the Colonel,
walking between tables, offering advice,
always laughing, setting everyone
at ease but me.

Texts with Geneva

Alicia: have you ever had sex with guys

Geneva: I've never had sex with anyone lol

Alicia: do you hate that I've had sex with guys?

Geneva: how could I hate anything about you?

Alicia: it's easy actually lol

Geneva: Stop.

Geneva: Have you always liked girls?

Alicia: Yes. Boys too. Sometimes I wish I didn't.

Geneva: I understand that without any context. You know what I hate?

Alicia: I've never heard you say "hate" before so I'm intrigued

Geneva: Ha. No, I hate when people ask me how I know I'm a
lesbian if I haven't had sex with anybody yet

Alicia: IYKYK

Geneva: If you know you know.

Texts to self

Alicia: do you regret having sex with guys?

Alicia: only when it was regretful. when it felt—what's that word Dr. Kareem used that one time? That means like something is mandatory, even if no one told you it was a rule?

Alicia: compulsory

Alicia: compulsory

Alicia: only then?

Alicia: Then. And when it feels like an escalator out of my head. When instead of an adventure into cricket song, touch is a cave I disappear inside. When it's the point of a pin dragged across secret skin. When shame is an echo echo echo

Alicia: I just want to be what I am. Whatever that is

Alicia: Seems simple

Alicia: I feel like it could be

Be what I am

Deja, untouched,
and me, no inch untouched

someone gazing from afar
might see opposites
    compulsory twoness

It feels like I am back
at the optometrist,
everything snapping
into crisp black focus:

We are not two sides
of a flat spinning coin

We are a ball turning
in the palm of a sun-warmed hand

We are traveling through
space

We both exist outside
any container
that seeks to hold us
We are both
made of blinding
light

I've never been to the coach's office

since it became Coach Tinsley's. It still has
all the plaques won under Coach Young—I guess
they belong to the school and not her.

Coach is at his desk on the phone when I walk in.
His eyebrows raise when he sees me, like he's a ghost hunter
finally getting an apparition on camera.

I stand by the door until he hangs up, and when he does
he tells me to sit down. I am wary still
of the door, of its potential to close. I don't know
him, don't trust the mouth that looks empty of fangs
but may be hiding them under those square human teeth.
    What can I do for you, Alicia?

I'm going to run, I say.
    Today?

Yes.
    Well . . .

Can I run?
Sure you can

Dr. Kareem looks sad when we enter for our group.

She usually has all her words warm and ready
but today she's searching for them
in the corners of the room, on the ceiling,
and when she eventually speaks she says

I'm so sorry, but this is our last meeting. I've been informed that our
conversations are inappropriate and I'm being
asked to continue my research observing your classrooms rather than in
this room
with you
alongside you
in community with you
and girls I am so sorry

but before she can finish, Annika is crying

it's my fault
it's all my fault
my brother told my dad
that I was kissing my boyfriend
and we got in a fight
and I told him what you said
about hymens, that it's all
an invention, that everything
I'm supposed to feel bad about
is like a ghost story at Girl Scout camp,
and he didn't hear me
he didn't see me

he just said he was going to call
the school and put a stop
to all of this.

When Dr. Kareem smiles, I'm surprised

because I don't feel like smiling, and Annika is still crying
Eugenia's arm around her shoulders. Deja's eyes
are shining wet, scowling. Everyone's faces are doing different
    things,
we are feeling different things, but we all know one thing
to be true: something has been taken from us.

Cry now, Dr. Kareem says, *it's okay to grieve a loss*
when it happens, but know that we have already won
because we had this, and will have this.
You have felt what it's like to be in community
with one another, to give names
to the things that hurt us.

What has happened is a tale
as old as time: sever mouth
from ear when freedom is whispered
              spoken
                    shouted

But what do we say to them
before we part?

We say: you were too late.
You were too late!
We have already heard each other!

Dr. Kareem asks us what makes us angry

and everyone has an answer.

Boys/men staring at our chests when we speak, mispronouncing our
    names, sometimes
      on purpose
bra strap snapping, be good at everything, sexy and innocent
    simultaneously

take up just enough space, aware of who's watching, always watching
    our brothers do what we're not allowed
you're too pretty not to smile
    what's there to smile about, asshole?
watch that pretty mouth

Women athletes at the Olympics getting fined for covering up but
    in high school
we get expelled for not covering up
        more.

You want sex you can't want sex why don't you want more sex no
    not that kind of sex no not that
either what do you mean you don't want sex at *all* your entire being
    is defined by sex

the boys who slur about hijab but ask with secret smiles to see the
    hair underneath, white girls who
say we're all in this together but *together* means using brown girls'
    backs as a bridge

Black girls like goddesses
Black girls like heroes
Black girls like mules
Black girls like angels until they're too angry

Black girls everything but   girls
Black girls like Simone Biles
    never allowed to say no

everyone with an opinion about skin skin skin

a) too much makeup b) you look so tired c) stay out of the sun,
    brown girl, before you get browner d) don't you want to cover
    your pimples e) why do you *have* pimples you're supposed to be

perfect
perfect
perfect

why are you so mad why are you so sad why are you so quiet why
    are you so loud . . .

So we get louder.

And Dr. Kareem encourages us:

Scream it. Say what makes you angry.
It's just us:
be as loud as you want

and we're timid at first—
still afraid of taking up too much space,

but Deja catches my eye
with hers, still wet with tears:
she is mortar, pestle
dynamite, match.
She is boat and river.
She is traveling
and I want to meet her. As we

scream the names of things
that tear us down, I promise
the air that I will be brick—
I will be brick and not wind,
not a drop in the slow hurricane
that erodes her grain by grain.

Louder, says Dr. Kareem, and asks

are we still afraid
of what our voices might accomplish
if we unleash them?

Maybe
but one by one we do
and if anyone is passing in the hall
they might think that someone
released a pack of wolves
and maybe
they would be right.

Walking through the halls

I can still hear the howling in my head

but more than that I hear rustling—

I feel like a snake shedding its skin

inch by

      papery

        inch

sliding it off as I become

something

new.

I find Deja in the library

buried in the stacks, burrowed deep
in new pages. The bell will be ringing
soon, sending us all outside.

When I sit down beside her,
she doesn't look up from her book.

I can't see the cover, but
AUDRE LORDE is in the margin,
Deja's finger stopped on the page.
I've read this poem,
"A Litany for Survival."

It is better to speak,
I read. *It is better to speak.*

Deja whispers, maybe because
we're in the library, or maybe
because it feels like a secret:

*Sometimes I feel like I'm dancing
on the edge between fury
and joy*

and I can tell she's not ready
to say more, so I just lay my head
on her shoulder, and she
rests her chin on top.

I murmur some of what
my mom told me:

It can all turn a human into a volcano.
I want you to know I'm here.
I can stand your lava.

Elsewhere in the library,
pages rustle and people sneeze.
Feet cross the carpet and people laugh
when they're not supposed to.
Twenty feet away, Blake told me
her truth. Here, there are a thousand books
to learn from and a thousand books
to unlearn.

When the bell rings, neither of us move.

They won't let me check this out, Deja says eventually,
laughing low. *I have too many fines.*

Fuck the fines, I whisper,
and we walk out with the book
tucked under my shirt.

I'm wearing last year's shoes but they feel different.

My feet haven't grown
but something else
has.

I feel bigger than I've ever felt
like every step might crack
the pavement

and when I pass the Colonel's classroom
on the way outside
I pause for a full minute.

He's not there.
He's in the cafeteria preparing
for the science fair
and I don't dare step in
through that always-open door

but I do look,
and I'm seeing more
than plastic arteries
and ceramic bones

I'm seeing my bones,
watching them rise
and walk to the track.

I remember the thing
that I saw on Tumblr,
how people with trauma
will sometimes reexpose
themselves to it,
salt in the wound
to stay alive.

I am tired
of salting the wound—
I am ready
to salt the earth.

Jacob Wheeler sees me first

and starts to walk to meet me, before pausing
hands half-raised. He thinks I am wild,
that approaching too fast might
run me off, a torch in the eyes
of something creeping from the forest.

He isn't wrong. Stepping out
onto the track makes me feel
exposed—even in long pants
and a hoodie, my skin feels
bare, the stands full of eyes.
Deja is there, and Geneva,
and they offer thumbs-ups
and waves, and smiles
made small in case they scare
me off. Everyone thinks
I'm on edge. They aren't wrong.

You're here, Jacob says,
and I nod. *Are you ready?*
I nod again. Words seem
like too much. He has plenty:
he tells me Coach has already
registered me for two events,
that my name is on the ledger.

Soon I'll be at the line,
soon I will be asked to run,
soon I will be asking myself
to fly.

I didn't call my mother

but Coach Tinsley must have.
I see her in the stands,
far from Geneva and Deja
because she doesn't know

they exist—she thinks
Sarah is the only friend
I had, that with all
the swimming I have done
through purple-dark water,

I have been swimming
alone. I gaze at them
from the starting line

and I realize just how wrong
we both have been.

"Runners on their marks"

The call comes, and I'm still looking
to the bleachers. That's how I see the cars
pull up, dark blue and official,
and the people stepping out of them,
the same serious navy.

No sirens, no lights,
but Blake is there
beside a woman with hair
like a jar of pennies
wild like snakes.

We are all here
and my throat is full
of hissing breath.

Daughter and mother
Deja and Geneva
Lena and Eugenia
girls and girls and girls

We are all here:
some center
of the universe drawing us
all together before we become
combustible—all that we are
exploding into the fury
of what we will become.

I can hear Blake's mother
howling. Soon mine
will be too. My brimming throat
is aching to empty.

We are all here, I think.
Here we go.
And there goes the pistol.

My legs are my own

and they can fly.
The sky is the color of March
turning to April, the bricks
are the same color
they have always been.

I am running
like I have always
been.

I am running away
from wolves
and gray rooms
and hidden teeth

from grease stains
and Bibles
and weed and cats

and I am running away
from plaster bones
and wooden hearts
and Cincinnati

I am even running away
from clipboards
and blue cars

but the track is a stretching circle
and it will bring me back—
it lets me run away
and back
at the same time.

In this moment,
my lungs
are breaking—how
can I speak when I can't
even hold air—but
at the end
of this circle

I think I will
be brave enough
to breathe.

Dear cave,

Dear grass,
Dear shadow,
Dear pit,
Dear bosom,
Dear boy,

I hope you find this letter
written in the sand
the words shaped
by the movement
of my body

the trail suddenly ending
as I remember
that a monster
is made of imagination
    and I take flight.

You will find me
where the sword is made

You will find me
where the shield is forged

You will find me
with my feet already wearing
the winged shoes

You will find me
shredding the cloak

All the gifts given
by the gods
breaking
in my teeth.

I am flying to Olympus
and I'm not coming alone.
    Sincerely,
    Medusa

Acknowledgments

My mother has always believed me, and for that I thank her. Omaun has always believed me, and for that I thank him. Hope has always believed me, and for that I thank her. Jessica has always believed me, and for that I thank her. Jerrica has always believed me, and for that I thank her.

There aren't many of you who believed me. For those who did, I thank you.

I have never written these kinds of acknowledgments before. This book was hard to write. If you read Alicia's story and you believe her, I thank you.

I am so incredibly lucky that this book found its way into the hands of Liesa Abrams, my cherished editor. I thank my agent, Patrice Caldwell, for finding it the perfect home, where it has been loved through its evolution by Liesa Abrams, Emily Harburg, and the other incredibly caring and sensitive hands at Labyrinth Road who saw and honored all of Alicia Rivers and her story. I remember sending two books to Patrice for consideration, this being one of them—I was so sure she'd run in the other direction. Patrice, I owe you so much. Thank you.

I reserve special thanks for Lucie Brooks, Asha French, and Ashley Woodfolk, who read this book in stages when it was lava pouring out of me. I never thought the words in these pages would see the light of day, but these women refused to let it (or me) hide. I can't believe I did this. Thank you for holding my hand through this catharsis.

I am grateful also (deeply) to Sherronda Brown and Viveca Shearin, whose loving words helped push this book farther toward revolution. Thank you, Junauda Petrus, for writing *The Stars and the Blackness Between Them,* which showed me what books for young adults can and should do—it guided me on the journey toward *Medusa.* Thank you, Samira Ahmed, for your kind and critical eye; you revealed more of this story and its girls to me. Thank you, Gabrielle Union, for your unending fearlessness and love.

Thank you, Audre Lorde.

Thank you, Marie Howe.

Thank you, Anne Sexton.

Thank you, Laurie Halse Anderson.

Thank you, Alice Walker.

Thank you, Sharon Olds.

Thank you, Lucille Clifton.

Thank you, believers.

Thank you, listeners.

Thank you, little Olivia, for refusing to die.

Note for Readers

To any readers who need resources on sexual violence,
the National Sexual Violence Resource Center
is a place to start looking for help:
nsvrc.org